PARKER
FIELD

OTHER BOOKS BY HOWARD OWEN

A WILLIE BLACK MYSTERY

PARKER FIELD

HOWARD OWEN

THE PERMANENT PRESS
Sag Harbor, NY 11963

For information, address:
  The Permanent Press
  4170 Noyac Road
  Sag Harbor, NY 11963
  www.thepermanentpress.com

Library of Congress Cataloging-in-Publication Data

Owen, Howard—
    Parker Field : a Willie Black mystery / Howard Owen.
      pages cm
    ISBN 978-1-57962-361-6
      1. Sportswriters—Fiction. 2. Baseball players—Fiction.
    3. Murder—Investigation—Fiction. 4. Sports stories. I. Title.

PS3565.W552P37 2014
813'.54—dc23   2014007556

Printed in the United States of America

As always, to Karen

Chapter One

THURSDAY, APRIL 5

*T*here was only one shot. Everybody was in agreement on that.

Nobody knows why he was in the goddamn park. Early April felt more like the middle of March. The wind stung like an inside pitch on an aluminum bat. Even the usual suspects wearing somebody else's clothes were hanging out around the homeless shelters or hunkered down where the sun could reach them but the wind couldn't. A week before, it had been eighty degrees. A balloon stuck in a tree and an abandoned Frisbee attested to Richmond's faithless spring weather.

I wasn't there. Mal Wheelwright had called a staff meeting at two, and attendance was not voluntary. These days, staff meetings are never called to announce we're getting raises and adding to staff. No refreshments are served. Still, you don't want to be counted "absent" and find your ID card doesn't work the next day.

This one was relatively painless. We're reducing the business section to three days a week to save newsprint. No jobs lost this time, Wheelie assured us, but the business news reporters and editors don't look so sure. Might be a good time to take that PR job, guys.

So I was in the newsroom when Sally Velez got the word. The police radio is pretty worthless these days. We get most of our tips from Twitter or our "friends" on Facebook, which is where this one came from. Sally was seated at her desk, half listening to Wheelie drone on about doing more with less while she scoured the electronic waterfront.

"Shit," I heard her say. I walked over and saw the tip: *Shots at monroe park. man down. what's up.*

"Better check it out," she said.

Chip Grooms from photo and I were more than happy to skip the rest of the meeting, now that we knew we weren't losing our jobs, taking pay cuts or getting more "furlough" days.

Since I had walked to the paper, we took Chip's car. We parked next to the Prestwould, where I live, and crossed the street. Ninety percent of the ether tips we get lead nowhere, but this looked like the one in ten that beat the odds. An ambulance and six squad cars were in and around what was obviously a crime scene, having driven over the grass's first pitiful efforts to paint the park green again.

I spied my favorite doughnut-eating flatfoot and walked up, hoping to get inside the yellow tape.

"Damn, Gillespie," I said. "I didn't know they made pants that big."

"Fuck you, Black," he said by way of greeting.

Then I saw the body.

I ran past Gillespie before he could catch me, and two other cops had their hands on each of my arms, trying to haul me away before I convinced them that the man on the ground was a friend of mine.

They were putting Les onto the stretcher. At first, I thought he was gone. But then I called his name, and he opened his eyes and looked at me.

"Willie," he said. "What the fuck?"

Chapter Two

FRIDAY

*F*or once, I don't need the alarm. I've been up since six, an hour I rarely see in the A.M.

Yesterday was wall-to-bleeping-wall.

I rode in the ambulance, almost getting arrested before the EMTs relented. I reached Peggy on the cell phone on the way to the hospital and told her, as gently as I could, that Les had been shot, but that he was OK, he was going to be fine—something that I wasn't in the least sure of. As I looked down at Les, lying there, with two guys trying to keep him from bleeding out, his eyes blinking at me but not definitely registering what was going on, I figured lying was my best strategy.

"What hospital?" Peggy yelled three times before I could cut through the hysteria and tell her.

"VCU. The big one."

She hung up in the middle of my baseless assurances. Neither my mother nor Awesome Dude, the guest who never left, has a car. They and Les usually depend on feet or buses or the occasional taxi—or, if all else fails, me and my hard-ridden Honda—to get them where they need or want to go. I wondered how she was going to get to the hospital, but I was focused on Les.

They separated him from me for a few minutes after they wheeled him in. Even in Richmond, shooting victims get the kind of prompt attention that the medical profession rarely affords us, and a small army of competent people whisked Les away to try and save his life.

By the time they let me come back, they had him sedated, which meant Les was more addled than usual. He's been slipping into some kind of dementia for the last three years at least, and the combination of being shot in the shoulder by what seems to have been a high-powered rifle, finding himself surrounded by a horde of strangers and being heavily medicated was making him a little wild.

By the time I got to his bedside, he was trying to rip the damn tubes out and get vertical.

I said his name four or five times before he finally looked at me, blinked twice and said my name, repeating the same question he'd asked me in Monroe Park.

I didn't know any other way to say it.

"Somebody shot you."

"Who?"

I had to tell him I didn't know. No one saw anybody anywhere around him before he reportedly collapsed on the park bench like, well, like a man who had been shot. A student fifty yards away thought Les had had some kind of seizure, then called 911 when she got close enough to see the blood.

"You're going to be OK, though," I told him, continuing my policy of constructive lying. I persuaded the nurses not to strap him down, assuring them this would only make his confusion and terror worse.

They rolled him up to his private room as I followed. I was having flashbacks to the scary time last year when Andi, my daughter, spent several days up here after getting T-boned by a careless driver. There are few places I'd less rather be than a hospital.

A doctor came in and asked me if I was a relative. I told him yes, which isn't much of a lie. Les Hacker has been more of a husband to Peggy than her three actual, legal husbands were, and saying he's been more of a father than my asshole stepdads is damning him with very faint praise.

I walked out in the hallway. Just because Les was addled and had lost a couple of quarts of blood didn't mean he was deaf.

I asked the question everyone asks when someone they love is hanging by a thread. "Is he going to be all right?" really means, "Please, please, save him."

The doctor didn't jump right in with a hearty affirmative.

"He needs some time to recuperate. He's had a terrible shock to his system. We'll know more in a couple of days."

I explained to him, as quickly as I could, that Les sometimes isn't hitting on all cylinders upstairs.

"Has he been seen by a specialist?"

No, I told him, we've been meaning to, but . . .

"Well," he said, looking a little impatient, "we'll need to look into that, too. We have some medications we can give him."

I figured the meds were going to be more to make Les behave than to really help him, but I wasn't sure giving the good doctor medical advice was going to be in Les's best interests.

The doc said he'd look in on him later.

"Don't worry," he said, in an almost-human show of sympathy. "He's in good hands."

I'd barely gotten back in the room when I heard Peggy down the hall, being loud.

"Les Hacker," she said, using her outdoor voice. "H-A-C-K-E-R. Am I going too fast for you?"

I retrieved her before they called security. Awesome Dude was with her, looking almost as stoned as Peggy. At first I didn't recognize the other guy and then realized it was Jerry Cannady, Peggy's neighbor and Oregon Hill's official pain in the ass. I figured Peggy must have been really desperate to get here in a hurry.

I thanked Jerry for driving them to the hospital. He grunted something like "you're welcome." I don't guess I ever apologized for threatening to pinch Jerry's head off and shit down his neck last year after he made such a fuss about Les's increasingly erratic behavior. Maybe I'll do it later. Apologize, I mean.

Abe Custalow, my corenter at the Prestwould, came and got us when it was time to go. When we left the hospital, Les was "resting comfortably." Peggy looked about as close to crying as I'd ever seen her. I had to convince her that staying by his bedside all night might not be good for her health or his, that he needed to sleep.

My mother has bid soon-to-be ex-husbands adieu with no evident regrets beyond wondering how we would pay the rent. (Usually, she could pay it better without them.) But I know Les is the one she doesn't want to get away. Even now, even while he isn't always sure where he is or where he's going, he adds some kind of crazy stability to my mother's house, perhaps because he's the only one there who isn't always stoned.

Theoretically, Peggy and Awesome Dude could go off the wacky weed and be a lot more dependable than Les. Theoretically.

AFTER I dropped them off, promising that we'd go back again today, and every day, as long as it takes, I went back to the office and wrote my story.

"He's your mother's, what, boyfriend? Jesus," Sally Velez said. "How old is your mother?"

I told her Peggy's as old as she'll be some day, if she's lucky.

"Do you think they're still . . . you know."

I told Sally to mind her own business.

I dropped by the hospital later, but Les was sleeping. I sat and watched him sleep for a couple of hours, then went home. I heard Penny Lane Pub call my name as I drove by, but for once I ignored its siren song. I've only recently become entitled to drive our streets again for anything other than work, fallout from my having been apprehended by our finest last year while trying to drive back from Penny Lane to the Prestwould, eleven blocks west, on an eastbound street, then spectacularly failing a sobriety test.

Chuck Apple had volunteered to cover for me on cops last night. His reward, I see in my morning paper that whacked against my door sometime after five, was a double-homi on the South Side. There's only a short on it on B1, which means it happened after ten, but Chuck probably had to spend half the night sending out tweets and Facebook postings and updating the tablet version of our creaking, wheezing rag. I owe him one.

The suits are sure the tablet is the answer, that we can get the suckers—er, readers—to pay to read us on their iPads and such, since they sure as hell aren't going to pay for our website after we've given it away for free there for more than a decade.

Putting stories on the tablet requires a lot of extra typing and clicking and dragging. They probably could train monkeys to do it for bananas, but the brain trust would rather have professional copy editors and night editors do it, giving them less time to—what's the word I'm trying to think of? Oh, yeah: edit.

Enos Jackson says he would like to give tablets to the suits. Cyanide.

Les's shooting is above the double-homi on B1. This is partly because the double-homi happened late, but partly because Monroe Park is more or less on the Virginia Commonwealth University campus and Les is white.

I drive over to Oregon Hill. The weather, fickle as ever, has turned from late winter to full-blown spring overnight. Along Laurel Street, the camellias are blooming and the trees seem to have turned into a yellow-green canopy, shading the sidewalks their roots are slowly destroying. Everything looks better on a warm day, I guess, although Les's condition is a cloud that kind of mocks all the beauty.

I see R. P. McGonnigal's Jeep Cherokee parked in front of Peggy's. With Jerry Cannady spreading the word, I'm sure everyone on the Hill knows about Les by now.

I give my old friend a man hug and thank him for stopping by. Several neighbors have brought over various casseroles and baked goods, which Peggy and Awesome seem to have already tucked into. A banana pudding seems to have been decimated, hapless victim to the munchies.

"What the hell happened?" R. P. asks me.

I tell him I'm damned if I know. Yesterday, the cops were still trying to figure out where the shot came from. After that, maybe they can tell us who would want to try to kill, or at least maim, a 79-year-old ex-minor-league catcher and roofer who, to my knowledge, didn't have an enemy in the world.

Out Peggy's front window, two kids who should be in school are walking up Laurel, throwing a baseball to each other as they go, keeping a desultory eye out for traffic.

"This would be a great day to take in a game," R. P. says, knowing full well that we both have other responsibilities. "Birds are home. Afternoon game. We could be there in time to have a couple of Nat Bohs at one of those little bars next to the stadium . . ."

"Stop it."

It is a perfect day for what McGonnigal suggests. The notoriously inaccurate weather page we run in the paper said seventy-five degrees and sunny, and it looks like maybe we got it right for once. If Les weren't in the hospital, I swear I'd call in well, get in the Cherokee and be off to Baltimore.

R. P. sighs.

"Yeah, I know. We must be a couple of old farts. We wouldn't have thought twice, a few years ago."

"Maybe twenty years ago."

"Aw," R. P. says, "not that long. When did we go to Bo Brooks for crabs that time, in the middle of the week, day kind of like this, maybe a little later in the year, then scalped those tickets down the third-base line?"

I tell him I think it was 1995.

"See? That was just . . . Shit, seventeen years ago. How did it get to be 2012?"

I tell him I don't have a clue. It did seem like we used to get away once or twice a year to see the Birds, and the less planning involved, the better. It was like throwing down a flag on the top of Mount Don't-Give-A-Shit and laying claim to the youth that all logic indicated had passed you by like a runaway freight train.

"One of these days," I tell him. "We'll do it again, I swear. Soon."

"Well," R. P. says, looking at his watch. "If you're going to pussy out on me, I guess I'd better get my ass to work."

R. P. works for an ad agency. I can't remember which one, because it's a different one every time I see him. He's smart and I'm guessing pretty valuable, but an ad agency might be a less stable place to work than even a daily newspaper newsroom. The wind shifts, and twelve people lose their jobs.

I walk him to the door. He's already in his Cherokee when I remember I should have asked him about his latest "friend," partner, whatever. The idea that R. P. McGonnigal, bosom friend of my misspent youth, is playing for the other side kind of throws me sometimes. I hope it doesn't show. Shit, I just want for R. P. what I want for just about everybody. I want him to be happy.

The only neighbors who are still there leave. I go into the kitchen, to help Peggy wrap things up and refrigerate anything that might spoil.

"Damn," she says, as we do a little triage and figure out what has to be either pitched or sent home with me, "you'd think somebody died."

As she says it, there's a little hitch in her voice. I put my arm around my mother and tell her everything's going to be all right.

Awesome Dude, who has been down in his English-basement living space and appears to have even showered and shaved, comes in and awkwardly puts his arms around both of us. On a normal day this nice, Awesome would have headed over to the park or gone down to the river to reunite with old acquaintances who haven't been as fortunate as he has. Stepping back and watching him comfort Peggy, though, I'm thinking that my mother has gotten more out of her generosity than just somebody to smoke dope with. Awesome has a roof over his head when he wants one, and Peggy has somebody to share her pain.

BACK AT the hospital, Les is in and out of consciousness. It's hard to tell how much of it is just Les and how much is the work of some of our more potent pharmaceuticals.

He thrashes about a bit, and a lot of what he says is incoherent. But then he'll look up at Peggy and tell her everything's OK, that he'll be home before she knows it.

The doctor comes by while we're there. He's still playing it pretty close to the vest, afraid to promise more than he can deliver. It's OK for me to assure my mother that Les will be all right. If I'm wrong, nobody will sue me for malpractice.

Les is still not quite clear on what happened, but then neither are we. I've checked with the police, and they're still trying to figure it out. The Richmond cops have plenty to do above and beyond figuring out how somebody almost got killed. There are plenty of successful homicidists out there. This one will get some attention, though. Most of the bullets that hail down on our fair city do not land in an area frequented by college kids.

Peachy Love, my favorite police flack and occasional whoopee partner, says they're still working on the angle of trajectory and all that bullshit. One thing she said, though, got my attention.

"This is totally off the record, Willie," she said. "You can't print this. You can't even talk about it, or my ass is in a sling, and I'll never talk to you again."

Not being able to talk to Peachy Love again would be a great loss to me. I promise, crossing my heart and hoping to die.

"It looks like it came from somewhere up high. It's not that easy to figure, and these guys aren't geniuses, but what one cop told me was the investigators think the perp must have been shooting down at the victim."

"What direction?"

"That one they're sure of. The shooter was to the north of him."

There are a couple of high-rise dorms just down the street, but they'd be a little out of range. Unless the bastard was perched in a tree, there's one tall building, all twelve stories of it, just to the north of Monroe Park.

The Prestwould.

Chapter Three

SATURDAY

The chairs they provide for hospital visitors are made to encourage short stays. The one I'm sitting in is the least comfortable of the two Les's room has been allotted. Peggy has the one right beside the bed. Every fifteen minutes or so, I use one excuse or another to take a walk.

Les is hanging in there. He's not the same old Les, though. The disorientation, the drugs, the damn trauma of being shot are all working against him. He thrashes around. He complains a lot, and I'm not sure I've ever heard Les Hacker complain before this. He pretty much knows who we are, but when Peggy and I look at each other, and we're sure he's not looking at us, I am certain that we do not brim with optimism.

It's a ten-minute walk to the nearest nicotine zone, so I'm doing more walking than sitting. I think I'd rather walk ten miles than spend an uninterrupted hour in a hospital room.

Out on the deck, it's turned cooler again. I'm tucked into a corner, out of the wind, when I hear my name being called.

"Willie! Hot damn, don't you know that shit'll kill you?"

I stub out my Camel and greet the tireless Jimmy Deacon. Jumpin' Jimmy Deacon. He actually refers to himself that way sometimes, in the third person. He's done it ever since Buddy Hicks, one of our sports writers, called him Jumpin' Jimmy in a feature story probably twenty years ago.

The nickname fits. Jimmy must be seventy-five now, and he's still working as much as they'll let him. Or can stand him. Jimmy would make the Sphinx jumpy. He has, since I've known him, had the energy level of a hummingbird. Unfortunately, he also has the brain of one. He's had one job or another involving Richmond and baseball for his entire adult life, none of them paying for much beyond his rent and groceries. In what he calls the off-season, between the end of the minor-league season and spring training, he referees, he keeps score at high school and small-college basketball games. He even worked as a stringer for the paper for a while, covering prep basketball, until someone realized that Jimmy couldn't read and write very well.

I read in the paper the other day that his title now is assistant groundskeeper. That's probably as good a fit as anything. The main thing with Jimmy, as any number of general managers will tell you, is to keep him busy. If you can find the right treadmill to put him on, one that keeps him busy and accomplishes something, he will work until he drops.

Jimmy looks like he weighs about 120 pounds. Somebody said he ran a 10K a couple of years ago, wearing a pair of work shoes, and finished in under fifty minutes. Somebody asked him how much he'd trained.

"Why the fuck would Jumpin' Jimmy run another six miles just for practice?" was the reported response.

"How's Les?" Jimmy asks me. We're face-to-face now, and Jimmy seems to be kind of vibrating. His red hair has faded to a weak yellow, but his bright blue eyes still shine, powered by some internal generator that doesn't seem to have an off switch. As much as I dislike sitting in a hospital room, I can't imagine Jumpin' Jimmy Deacon lasting five minutes.

I tell him Les is doing well.

"Well, I come to see him."

I see that Jimmy has some roses in his right hand. They aren't in a vase. They look like he bought them at the grocery store on the way over.

"I figure they'll have something to put 'em in," Jimmy says when he sees me staring at the flowers. A thorn seems to have cut Jimmy's hand, which is bleeding a little. Still, it was a nice thought.

"Who the hell would want to shoot Les?" Jimmy asks. "Jumpin' Jimmy never knew a better fella. Some of those ballplayers, I tell you, they can be kind of high-hatted sometimes, you know? But Les wasn't ever like that."

I knew Jimmy before I knew Les but didn't really get to know him until Les and Peggy hooked up. He and Les have been friends for almost half a century, since Les caught for the Vees and Jimmy was whatever he was at the time—clubhouse guy, ticket seller, advance man, peanut vendor. At one point many years after Les retired, he and Jimmy would share the duties of warming up the pitchers in the bullpen. In the big leagues, they have an actual catcher doing that. In the minors, it falls to anybody with a glove. So, either Jimmy or Les would put on a uniform—by then it was the Richmond Braves—and spend the game out in the area staked off along the right-field line for the relief pitchers.

Les said he kind of enjoyed it. He said he could still teach some of the young knuckleheads a thing or two. He said they wanted him to do it for every home game, because Jimmy's chatter was driving the whole bullpen crazy, in addition to which he loved to razz the opposing team's right fielder. One night, Jimmy got on this big goon from Toledo so bad that he went after him, right in the middle of the game, chased him all the way under the bleachers.

Les said he told the GM that thirty-five games were about all his knees could stand. He was probably fifty-five or sixty by then.

The main reason, though, was that he thought being replaced as bullpen catcher would have hurt Jimmy's feelings.

Jimmy and I agree that we can't think of anyone who would want to shoot Les Hacker.

"Musta been a case of mistaken identity," Jimmy says, and I have to concur.

We're walking back into the VCU hospital, with Jimmy talking all the way.

"Les is luckier than some. Those '64 boys, they kinda had a hard time of it."

I figure he means the 1964 Richmond Vees. Les has told me how Jimmy seems to remember all the players on all the Richmond teams, no matter how obscure they are, as if all of Jimmy's scant brain cells have been focused on that one thing.

"What do you mean?"

"Well, Lucky and Phil, the only ones that made it to the bigs, they're both gone."

Jimmy stops and rubs the knot over his right eye.

"Damn!" he says. "I'm just remembering. They both were shot, too. Damn!"

I remember Lucky Whitestone, because he was the most famous member of the 1964 team. He made the All-Star team two or three times in the majors, I think. Almost led the league in hitting one year. I used to have his baseball card. I was four years old when he played his one season for the Vees, but everybody talked about him when I was growing up. Les still does. He said he had all the tools "and knew it, too."

"He died in some kind of hunting accident, right?"

"Yeah," Jimmy says. "He'd already retired. Had ten years in the majors. I heard he'd retired to Florida. Talladega, I think."

"Tallahassee?"

"Yeah. Yeah. That's it. They said he'd been deer hunting. They found him out there in the woods, shot through the head."

Jimmy stops for a couple of seconds and offers his final thoughts on Lucky Whitestone.

"He was a prick."

I ask him who Phil is, or was.

He looks at me as if I don't know who George Washington was.

"Phil Holt! He was a big old southpaw. From somewhere in Alabama. He won twelve games for the Vees in '64. Won fifteen for Detroit one year, before he threw his arm out."

"What happened to him?"

"I heard it was a holdup. He'd kind of pissed his money away. Hell, there wasn't that much back then anyhow. He was managing a 7-Eleven or some such shit, maybe he owned it, I don't know. This guy came in with a gun. Nobody else in the store but them, musta been late. Best they could figure, the guy just blew him away. They said he got about twenty dollars. I don't think they ever caught the son of a bitch."

So, yeah, Les could be a lot worse off.

"They were the only two that year that really did anything in the big leagues," Jimmy says.

I ask him how close Les had come to making it. Les always downplays his exploits, so it's hard to know.

Jimmy is quiet for a few seconds, which is rare.

"Oh, he coulda made it," Jimmy says. "If he hadn't been with the Yankees, there might of been opportunities. But they were full up on catchers. Les could hit a little, and he had a gun. They didn't run much on him. Best thing about Les, though? He could talk to the pitchers, get their heads on straight.

"You know that movie, 'Whispers to Horses'?"

"'The Horse Whisperer'?"

"Yeah. Whatever. Well, Les, he was the pitcher whisperer."

Up in Les's room, Jimmy hands the flowers to Peggy, who holds them for a few seconds and then sets them down gently on the bedside table.

Jimmy talks to Les for a few minutes. I can see him shifting from one foot to the other at the bedside. Les has the closest thing I've seen him have to a coherent conversation since he was shot. It's like seeing Jimmy Deacon has taken him back to an earlier time, when he wasn't addled and lying in a hospital bed with a ruined shoulder.

"You won't be throwing out many runners with that thing," Jimmy says, tapping Les's bandaged shoulder.

Les laughs and says he didn't throw that many out before he got shot, either.

"Aw," Jimmy says, "you did, too. You were a cannon back there."

By the time Jimmy leaves, all of ten minutes and a few thousand words after he arrived, Les seems to be feeling better.

Jimmy's barely out of earshot when I hear Peggy laugh.

"That man," she says, "just sucks all the air out of the room, doesn't he?"

I HAVE to be at work by three. I can't let Chuck Apple take another weekend night shift for me. As I'm leaving, I tell Peggy I'll pick her up and take her home in about three hours.

"Damn," she says, "I could use a smoke."

I know she doesn't mean tobacco. I tell her to hang in there.

"Easy for you to say. Your sins are all legal."

Mostly, I tell her.

In the parking lot, the cell phone buzzes. It's Kate.

She asks me about Les. It's the second time she's called. I appreciate her concern. My ex-wives have been kinder to me than I deserve.

I fill her in. She takes a breath and then dives in.

"I was going to call you anyhow. I didn't have a chance to tell you the other day. You had another call coming in, I think."

"Tell me what?"

"Well," she says, "the rabbit died."

It's such an old-fashioned phrase, especially from the decidedly new-fashioned Kate Ellis, that I don't get it for a couple of seconds.

"Oh, that rabbit."

The rabbit has been eluding Kate and her husband, Greg, for a couple of years. They have employed doctors and drugs and, for all I know, rhinoceros-horn emulsions in an effort to have a baby. Something finally worked.

I offer my congratulations, making a heroic effort to render them heartfelt.

"I feel kind of, you know, weird. But I didn't want you to hear it from someone else."

Kate and I never tried to have a baby. We tried not to have a baby. Or at least I'm sure I did. Kate was finishing law school and then getting her career started. I just wasn't into having another kid right then. Still, hearing the news is like hearing a distant door slamming. You walked away from it a long time ago, but there was always the hope that it might stay cracked just a bit. Kate and I did love each other. We just loved some other things, too, and in the end there wasn't enough love to go around.

We've become friends since we got over the initial unpleasantness, and we even managed to have one nostalgia fuck a year and a half ago that at least one of us doesn't regret in the least.

Still, the door is shut.

I ask her when, and she says probably October. The math says she's three months along.

"Remember that time we thought you were pregnant?" I kind of wish I hadn't said it as soon as the words are out of my mouth.

There's silence for a few seconds, and I'm afraid she's hung up the phone.

"It was probably for the best," she says at last.

Yeah. It wasn't one of my finer moments. After all, she was the one who was still in law school, the one who would have had to make some major changes in her bright career plans. But it had come as a shock to me. I thought we were being careful.

It was a mistake to ask if she'd skipped a birth control pill or six. It was a mistake to mention an abortion. It definitely was a mistake not to do the happy dance. After she finally had her period, there was a little bit of a chasm there, one I never succeeded in doing anything about but widening.

"You'll be a great mom," I tell her.

"And Greg will be a great father," she says, and I'm smart enough to know that I'm supposed to second that motion, no matter how much I think it's bullshit.

"Any news on who shot him?"

I tell her I don't have a clue. I feel like it's important not to breach Peachy's confidence and talk about the Prestwould angle. Besides, I'm sure the cops will spill their guts as soon as they have enough information to make it look like they're earning their doughnuts.

And, of course, she can't resist asking The Question:

"How about you and AA?"

"Next question."

She's been after me to "confront my problem" ever since the DUI that cost me my license for a while. I did try. I went to three meetings. But when they'd get to the part where I had to stand up and say, "Hi, I'm Willie, and I'm an alcoholic," I just couldn't do it. Dammit, I don't feel like an alcoholic. I still have a job, at least for the time being. I still have a functioning liver. I haven't had anyone have to tell me what I did the night before in months now. I know people AA has helped. No denying that. I just don't think I'm one of them.

Kate says I'm too stubborn. Maybe she's right. I tell her I've cut back to a fifth a day, which she doesn't think is terribly amusing.

I hear the dramatic sigh.

"Well, it's your life. Live it however you see fit."

I thank her for caring enough to nag.

She tells me to give Peggy and Les her love. I tell her to give Greg mine. She calls me a smart ass and hangs up.

ON THE way to the office, I call Andi. She's been by the hospital once already. She's working an early shift today at a place west of Boulevard that only sells food because the state says you have to if you want to sell liquor, too. Andi says it's so bad she's been helping out with the cooking. She's recovered from almost getting killed by an idiot driver eighteen months ago and is putting in four shifts a week plus taking three courses. It is possible that she and VCU will part ways sometime in the next year. She's really trying to pull her weight, tuition-wise, but my bank account will be a little less anorexic when she graduates.

She says she'll come by the hospital after work, and that she can pick up Peggy there and take her home.

My daughter is dating a guy who has rings in both nostrils and a stud on his tongue. She says he's really good to her, though, so who cares about rings and studs? Plus, he's old money, and maybe there's still some of it around. And he's bound to be better at relationships than I've been.

THE NEWSPAPER is in usual Saturday hibernation mode when I come in. It's hard to explain to civilians how Saturday is such a dead day around the newsroom.

"Isn't Sunday your biggest paper?" they tend to ask.

Yes, I explain. But if you look at what's in the Sunday paper, you soon realize that the only sections that can't be locked up on Thursday, or Friday at the latest, are the A section, the local section, and sports. All the feature stuff, the business pages, whatever bullshit the editorial writers have come up with, can be done ahead of time, and I guarantee you most of A1 and the local stuff is written and turned in before the sun sets on Friday. The Saturday crew is there to edit and write headlines. And, sometimes, actual news breaks out. The actual news tends to be of the criminal variety, which gets me out of the office.

I kind of like it. It's quiet in here for the most part, with the occasional shooting to break the monotony, and nobody's on your case, because anybody with a suit probably isn't even answering calls at home by Saturday afternoon.

Sarah Goodnight is at her desk on her day off.

She looks up when she sees me standing beside her.

I ask her why she's working for free.

"They had a brawl last night at Tredegar."

The American Civil War Center, one of our fair city's many efforts to turn the Late Unpleasantness into tourist dollars, is down by the James, in the old Tredegar Iron Works building.

Part of the exhibit is a video with paid talking heads trying to be fair and balanced, giving all sides. At one point, they ask you to press one of four buttons beside your chair, answering the burning question: What caused the Civil War?

Three boneheads from the South Side started arguing with the screen when it was revealed that the most common answer was, duh, "slavery." They were pretty sure the answer was "states' rights," as in states' rights to allow slavery. A few tourists from somewhere well north of the Potomac begged to differ, and it was on.

The museum folks obviously weren't thrilled to talk about it, but the room was apparently pretty much trashed, and anybody else who was there at the time couldn't have missed it. One of them called the paper last night, too late to get anything into today's paper. Sarah went over there this morning and found a college boy from VCU working the desk who told her most of the details. Sarah's getting good at persuading people to tell her things. She's especially good at it when they're of the opposite sex.

"I'd already checked with the police, and they arrested four of them, two from here, two from out of town."

"Seems fair," I offer.

"Think it'll make A1?"

"Probably local front."

I remind her that the tree-killing three-part series on the past, present and future of Richmond's riverfront takes up two-thirds of the front page and three more pages inside. Having an A1 story beside it on a brawl at a riverfront museum might be a bit more irony than our publisher could take.

"Oh, yeah," she says, rolling her lovely eyes. "Shit."

Sarah still wants people to read what she writes. She's twenty-six now and would like to be working at a larger paper somewhere. She has the brains and the A-personality for it. The fact that she's attractive, funny and hot as hell won't hurt her chances, either. I only hope there are some big-city dailies still breathing long enough for her to make a career out of this. Or, for her sake, maybe I don't. Sarah ought to go to law school. Lawyers don't do Saturdays and they don't work for free.

"How's your mother's friend doing?"

Like the rest of the newsroom, Sarah knows my link to Thursday's shooting.

She asks me what I know.

"Nothing so far," I tell her. "But I think the cops are close to making some kind of announcement."

"Yeah," she says, going back to her story. "Gillespie said tomorrow."

I talked to Gillespie yesterday, hoping he'd confirm or add to what Peachy told me. I've known him for thirty years. He had nothing. Like I said, Sarah's getting good.

The rest of my shift is almost too smooth. There isn't anything vaguely resembling a chance to leave the office on business, although I hop over on my dinner break to check on Les. Andi's still there, but she's about to leave with Peggy, who is showing her age after a day in the hospital.

I thank Andi for taking Peggy home. Les seems to be sleeping.

"The doctor didn't say much," Andi tells me. "He just said Les was 'hanging in there.'"

I just want to get Les home. He already looks like a different man, a husk of what he was three days ago. Les might have been losing it before the shooting, but a seventy-nine-year-old man who can still climb a ladder up to one of those Oregon Hill roofs, even if he's driven by dementia and thinks he's still running a roofing company, has a lot of juice. The Les before me looks like he's been pitted and seeded.

It's barely eleven thirty and I'm playing my last game of solitaire on the computer, ready to call it a night, when the phone rings.

I can barely hear Sarah's voice. I finally determine that she and some of our coworkers are at Penny Lane and intend to be there until they are forced to leave.

"Come on over," she yells into the phone. "They're asking about you."

I haven't been to my favorite pub much lately. It's part of the deal I've made with myself. No AA, but no Penny Lane, either, except on special occasions.

I try to demur, alluding to my need to go home, have some warm milk and low-fat cookies and go to bed.

"You're not gettin' old on me, are you, Willie?" Sarah says.

Well, Saturday night can be a special occasion.

Chapter Four

SUNDAY

$\mathcal{S}$arah Goodnight was right.

I am awakened by a call from Peggy, who tells me that someone from the police department called sometime before nine and gave her an update.

"They said the shots came from your building. They're going to have something about it on the news, the guy said."

I'm thinking it's a good thing they didn't come by Peggy's to tell her in person. You probably could smell the dope five feet outside the front door.

"Did they say what floor?"

"I think they said the ninth. Oh, Willie. Who'd want to shoot Les?"

To my knowledge, no one in the Prestwould is packing. I tell her I'll check into it.

I go to the newspaper's website. Sure enough, the police must have sent over a press release in the last hour or so. "Police closing in on shooter," is the headline put on it by the kid in charge of giving away free news.

The gist of it:

"Richmond Police Chief L. D. Jones said, that, based on forensic evidence gained over the last few days, it has been determined that the assailant fired one shot from a rifle from a window on the ninth floor of a dwelling at 612 West Franklin Street."

Home sweet home.

I lean out the bedroom window and have my first Camel of the day, making sure that none of the smoke stays inside. Kate, my landlady and last ex, would approve.

I hear voices above me. When I look up, there's the fat, sweaty face of Gillespie peering out a window three floors up. He looks down, sees me, and ducks his head back inside.

I swallow two aspirin with the coffee Custalow's already made for me. The night, as nights often do, turned out to be longer than expected. Three hours after I'd expected to be sleeping the sleep of the just, I was just getting in. Four of us went back to Sarah's place after Penny Lane kicked us out at closing time. Chip Grooms from photo and Becky Whitehouse, who covers prep sports, were there. They and Sarah might be seventy-five years old, combined.

When I left, they were still going strong. Sarah walked me to the door.

"Should you be driving?" she asked me, standing close enough that I could smell her perfume. "Maybe you ought to stay over. You don't need another DUI."

I was tempted to agree. I have been known to be very agreeable, especially with younger female employees.

I asked her for a rain check. She's barely older than Andi, my big brain whispered, but most of my big brain's victories are short-lived. And Sarah and I do have a bit of history, God forgive me.

I TAKE the utility stairs up to the ninth floor. I have forgotten whose unit it is until I open the door onto the foyer the two units in this tower share and come face to face with a piece of art that looks like somebody did projectile vomiting on the canvas.

Finlay Rand.

He's one of two art-and-antiques dealers living here. Most of what I know about Rand comes from Clara Westbrook, who makes it a point to know everybody and everything connected to the Prestwould.

"I like Finlay," she told me once, after a couple of Scotches. "He doesn't bother anybody, and that's about all I ask of my neighbors."

Rand is a confirmed bachelor, it seems, and Feldman, my nosy neighbor, conjectures that he might be a tad light in the loafers, but Clara said she knows for a fact that he has had overnight guests of the female persuasion.

"Besides," she added, "what's wrong with it if he does like men?"

Indeed, I said, and we toasted tolerance.

CRIME TAPE is across the open door to Rand's apartment. I duck under it and am halfway down the hallway when one of the cops, who looks like he's about nineteen, intercepts me.

"It's OK," I tell him. "I live here."

"You're . . ." he looks at his notes. "You're Finlay Rand?"

No, I explain to him, as I walk him the rest of the way to the living room—which has the best view of Monroe Park—I live in the building, not this particular unit.

"You shouldn't be here," he says, grabbing my arm.

A voice booms out behind me.

"He of all people shouldn't be here."

I turn to see my favorite flatfoot coming out of the kitchen.

"This jerk's a reporter," Gillespie tells his young associate. "What the hell did you let him in for? You think this is an open house?"

I tell Gillespie to get the stick out of his ass, that I'm off duty, just trying to find out what happened. I remind him that Les is practically family.

"How did they figure it was the ninth floor?" I ask Gillespie.

"The angle. These guys can figure out that shit. Math majors." He says it with the same tone he'd have used to say "pedophiles."

A lieutenant comes up. He's Gillespie's boss even though he looks like he's barely half his age, and he finds out I live in the building. He asks me if I know anything about Finlay Rand. I tell him that he's an antiques dealer.

"Do you know if he knew the victim?"

"I doubt it. Les wasn't much into antiques, unless maybe they were old baseball cards."

I explain to the lieutenant my connection to Les Hacker.

"He's a damn reporter," Gillespie says.

I tell the lieutenant that it's all off the record, that I'm just here because Les is family.

"I doubt if Finlay was the shooter," I tell them.

"How come?" Gillespie asks.

"He's on vacation. Won't be back until Wednesday."

Custalow told me. Rand asked maintenance to hold his mail until April 11. Said he was going to some place in the British West Indies for a month. Virgin Gorda, I think. Antiquing must be doing better than newspapers.

"Well," the lieutenant says, "somebody apparently broke in. Whoever it was must've used a silencer, because nobody heard anything. And he left everything here. Winchester .30-30, spent shell, everything."

I wonder out loud why he didn't shoot more than once, if he went to all that trouble.

"C'mere," Gillespie says, beckoning me to the window.

He points down to the park.

"See that big oak tree there?"

I nod.

"Well, when the victim got shot, he rolled forward, and that tree was between him and the shooter. He couldn't hit him, and we guess he didn't feel like he had a lot of time to waste up here."

"Les Hacker didn't have an enemy in the world," I tell them, "unless maybe it was some base runner he threw out trying to steal second in 1964."

"Well," the lieutenant says, "I'd say he had at least one, wouldn't you?"

I am warned that all this is on the QT. I promise not to publish it, but I don't promise not to tell Les and Peggy as much as I've been able to ferret out about this whole screwed-up affair.

I'm still there when the chief, L. D. Jones, shows up. His full name is Larry Doby Jones, named after the guy who was the first black player in the American League. Old farts like me, though, we still remember him from high school days as Long Distance Jones, second-team all-state guard from Maggie Walker. We go way back. These days, he looks like he's smelled spoiled meat every time he sees me. My second time around as night cops reporter has led to some unfortunate conflicts of interest between the chief and me. L. D. wants to keep every single detail of every case buried deep until he can call a press conference and do the we-got-him victory lap. I just want to get the story in the damn paper before I see it in living color on TV.

I tried to explain this to L. D. once, a couple of years ago. I was still able to draw on a small account of good will from my first stint as night cops reporter, thirty years ago, when the chief and I were both young pups who still could kid each other about my late black father making the two of us one-and-a-half African Americans.

"Why should I give it to the damn newspaper first?" he said. "You all are a dinosaur. I might as well send it out by Pony Express."

He seemed to think that was funny.

He's not laughing now.

"What is he doing here?" he says now by way of greeting.

The lieutenant tries to explain that I'm a relative, that this is all off the record. Gillespie slips into the kitchen, trying to make his fat ass invisible.

"I don't care if the victim was his got-damn daddy!" L. D. says, going into full James Earl Jones mode, bouncing up and down as he gets in the lieutenant's face. "Nothing's off the record with this son of a bitch. Get him the fuck out of here."

The chief doesn't even look at me as I leave.

I PICK up Peggy and Awesome Dude and take them over to the hospital. On the way, I give Peggy the news that Les seems to have been shot from the very building where I sleep, in the currently vacant apartment three floors up.

"The Prestwould?" she asks. "Those rich bastards don't go around shooting people."

"Rich bastards" is the way Peggy sees my fellow owners and renters. To her, the place seems like the Taj Mahal, with its Oriental carpet in the lobby and full-time staff. I have told her more than once that the place is full of widows on fixed incomes.

"Well," she said the last time we had this discussion, "I bet it's fixed a lot better than mine is. Social Security doesn't fix it too high, I can tell you that."

I assure my mother that the police are on top of it, that they've got the weapon and it's only a matter of time until they find out who shot Les.

"I hope they find out why, too," she says. I have to agree that I'm also kind of short on possible reasons.

"Ought to string the bastard up," Awesome adds.

Yeah, I agree. They should.

At the hospital, I'm surprised the nurses can't smell the marijuana that permeates my mother's clothes. The way they look at her, maybe they do. But she and Awesome are both more or less straight.

We don't have that much to talk about. Normally, I see Peggy once every week or two. Being together every day for several hours has already emptied the shallow reservoir of chat we might have been storing up.

Peggy mainly sits and holds Les's hand, talking to him when he's coherent and knows who she is, otherwise just sitting there. The TV is on, but she doesn't seem to be focused on much of anything.

I asked her once, years ago, why she and Les never married.

"Honey," she said, "I don't want to jinx it. Me and husbands don't have such a track record, you know?"

I know. The best adjective you could affix to any of my three stepfathers would have been "negligent." There were days I prayed for negligence. Oregon Hill in those days was a place where putting bread on the table—even if it was from the past-due-date store—gave you permission to administer tough love to kids, sometimes without the love.

Now, with the best man in her checkered adult life doing no better than "hanging in there," my mother looks old. It's all relative, I guess. She's almost seventy, and she's long had a weather-beaten look that she earned wrinkle by wrinkle. But she's always been lively, even when she was stoned. Now, though, her natural high-beam energy looks like it's down to about the level of a night-light.

I'm about to take my third smoke break in the last two hours when Jumpin' Jimmy Deacon, whose voltage has not been diminished in the least, comes vibrating into the room.

"Hey!" Jimmy says, jolting us out of our torpor. "How's the old Hacker doing? Ready to catch both ends of a doubleheader?"

Les opens his eyes and smiles at the sight of his old friend.

"Might need to warm up a little," he manages.

Jimmy dives into a discussion about the Flying Squirrels, whose home opener is on Thursday.

"The Rats look good," he says. "Got some talent coming up. Got some arms."

"Rats" is short for "Tree Rats," which is what Jimmy and other old-timers call the Double-A team that is Richmond's latest minor-league offering. Even the sports department balks at the tendency to name minor-league ball teams like they're characters in a Saturday morning kids' TV show. The sports guys have motives that are more selfish than aesthetic, though. The problem they have is that you can't get "Squirrels" into a one-column headline. Management has not yet approved using "Rats" in heads, as in "Rats/edge/Sens/in 10."

The Atlanta Braves pulled their Triple-A team out of here three years ago. They moved it to an Atlanta suburb, and we got demoted to Double-A.

You could see the train wreck coming ten miles away, but nobody put on the brakes. The city and the surrounding counties don't play well together on a good day. The counties owe most of their growth to white flight, leaving the urban centers to stew in their own juices in a state where it's almost impossible for cities to incorporate an inch of suburban top-soil. Parker Field evolved into The Diamond back in 1988, the previous time the parent club gave us a fix-it-or-lose-it prop-osition. Richmond and the counties buried the hatchet and built a new stadium together, but they didn't bury it forever, or even deep.

This time, the shakedown came in the midst of what feels like more than just a recession if you're not a trust-fund baby. When tax money started drying up, regional cooperation was the first thing to go. Several plans failed, some cooked up by greed heads who saw a way to make a buck with blue-sky schemes that promised a hell of a lot more than they could deliver. The city had no money, the counties pleaded poverty, and the R-Braves packed up and left.

It took about two minutes for the Giants to agree to move their Double-A team here from some beaten-down northeast-ern city with bigger problems than ours, and now we are the proud host city of the Richmond Flying Squirrels.

The kids love the mascot, Nutsy, and I guess that's the whole idea. I just hope they still love him when they're old enough to actually know the rules of baseball.

And, of course, the Giants brain trust already is harrumphing about the fact that we're not stepping lively to build them a new stadium.

If it weren't for the game itself, I'd have stopped following baseball a long time ago.

The Diamond does need a major makeover. It was built on the cheap and was (and still is) in need of either major renovations or dynamite. A chunk of concrete had been known to fall on the upper deck, although not, so far, on anyone's head. The visitors' locker room should be shut down by the health department.

"I think Nutsy's neat," Awesome offers. Jimmy just stares at him, speechless for once.

Jimmy and Les start talking about the old Vees. Jimmy does most of the talking. I'm afraid he's wearing Les out, but the old guy seems as animated as I've seen him since he was shot.

"Remember the time ol' Roy Haas told Rabbit Larue to just go up there without a bat and try to get a walk?" Jimmy says. "Rabbit was about oh-for-June, and he was in the on-deck circle."

"Yeah," Les says, so low you can barely hear him. "Rabbit was pissed."

"Guy before him strikes out, and there's still runners on first and third, two out. Haas is hitting behind Rabbit."

"How do you remember this stuff?" I ask Jimmy.

"Oh," Jimmy says, tapping his skull, "Jumpin' Jimmy don't forget nothin'. I got a pornographic memory."

"So then," he continues, "Haas says, 'Hey, Rabbit. Just leave the bat back here. Work him for a walk.' "

He and Les crack up, although the effort makes Les wince. Jimmy's wheezing, he's laughing so hard.

"So Rabbit turns around and charges Haas. He's got a bat, and so does Roy, who's got to outweigh him by fifty pounds. They look like The Two Mousketeers out there, like two kids sword fighting. I don't think either one of them made contact, which was about par for the course for Rabbit.

"The umpire didn't know whether to shit or go blind— excuse me, Ma'am. Finally, old Trent Julian—hell of a manager, old Trent was—he walks out of the dugout, spits a big wad on the field and says, 'Hey, ump. Throw 'em both out. I'm sick of 'em.'"

"Funniest thing was," Les says, in about the longest sentence I've heard him speak in the last four days, "Rabbit went four for four the next day."

"Three for four," Jimmy says, and Les yields to his superior knowledge of the 1964 Richmond Vees.

But Les knows something that Jumpin' Jimmy doesn't, pornographic memory and all.

"It's too bad about old Roy," he says.

"What?" Jimmy asks him.

"Heart attack. He died back in 2008, I think it was. Him and me exchanged Christmas cards every year. The only one I still kept up with. Him and Rittenbacker. And he's gone, too."

Jimmy fills us in on Jackson Rittenbacker.

"The Ripper," Jimmy says. "Him and Haas and Whitestone were about the only guys we had that year that could get it past the warning track. I didn't know he was gone, too. What happened?"

Les is starting to fade.

"I think he drowned," he says, and then he lies back, and I suggest that we let him get some rest.

"I'll be back soon," Jimmy says, grabbing his hand so hard that I'm afraid he'll dislodge the IV line. "We'll talk some more. Remember Frannie Fling? You can't talk about '64 without Frannie coming up."

Les opens his eyes and then shakes his head. And then he's asleep.

I walk Jimmy back out to his car. I need a smoke break.

"So Haas and, what, Rittenhouse, they're gone, too?"

"Rittenbacker. Hit fifteen home runs and struck out 138 times. Had a hole in his strike zone you coulda drove a truck through."

I'm thinking Jimmy's maybe an idiot savant, rather than just the first part.

"But, yeah, if Les said they're gone, they're gone. That's a shame. We're all getting old."

Not that old, I'm thinking. A thought sprouts in the arid landscape of my brain.

"It'd be interesting to do something on the old Vees. Readers eat up that whatever-happened-to stuff."

Jimmy snorts.

"Sounds like you better find some that's still above ground."

He's getting into a Chevy that looks like it's about one oil change from antique status.

I thank him for coming.

"Aw, it ain't nothing."

And then he tells me how Les, back when he ran a roofing company, paid most of Jimmy's hospital bills one winter when Jumpin' Jimmy had to have an emergency appendectomy and found out his health insurance with the team ended with the last out the season before.

"Les," he says, "he's a prince. I couldn't get him to take a cent for it. Must have cost him thousands, even back then. He's like that fella in the Bible, the good Sammerian."

"Samaritan?"

"Whatever."

"Oh," I ask Jimmy as he gets the Chevy to start on the third try. "Who was that you mentioned there at the end? Frannie somebody."

Jimmy shakes his head.

"Frannie Fling. Her real name was Frances Flynn. That's kind of a sad story. Maybe you can get Les to tell you that one when he wakes up. Whoa. Look at the time. Gotta go. Ain't got but four days to get that field ready."

And with that, Jumpin' Jimmy drives away. Through the exhaust fumes, I can see his head bouncing up and down, like a life-size bobblehead doll, like he's listening to some music that the rest of us can't hear.

Chapter Five

MONDAY

*B*uford "Bootie" Carmichael is sitting back fat and comfortable in his plush chair, talking too loud. Both the chair and Bootie dwarf their smaller, more streamlined peers. The other sports writers, who look like they all got together and ran a 10K before breakfast, are sitting in the ergonomically correct, cheap-as-shit chairs the company provides. As with raises, the suits are minimalist when it comes to office furniture.

Bootie's chair isn't standard issue. He picked it out and had it delivered to the sports department. Anyone who knows Bootie is pretty sure no money changed hands in the deal. The week after he ensconced his butt on his new throne, he wrote a column about how comfortable it was, praising the store that "sold" it to him. Bootie has been doing business like that since before I came to work here.

He's at least thirty years older than any of the other five reporters, three male and two female, who share the sports department with him this morning. I can't help but notice that the young lions' conversations tend to be very businesslike and to the point. Bootie, on the other hand, likes to ramble. Two of the other reporters are plugged in to iPods.

"The hell you say!" he roars for the third time, laughing so hard I'm thinking about giving him the Heimlich maneuver, if I could get his fat ass out of his chair long enough to do it.

I'm not sure any of his colleagues would bother with trying to save Bootie.

"He said he turned Clemson down because they served him shrimp, and he doesn't like shrimp? Well, what did you all serve him? . . . Yeah, I think I'd stay away from all kinds of shellfish, if I was you."

He talks for another five minutes. I gather the person on the other end is either some assistant coach Bootie's on drinking terms with or a jock-sniffing donor, and the other party is giving him the skinny on the latest high school moron Virginia Tech wants to pass off as a student-athlete. The schools that want to be "big time" in college football, meaning they get pounded by Top Ten teams instead of Podunk U, all have to save a few places in the freshman class for kids with "special talents." The talents usually trend toward 4.4 times in the forty-yard dash or thirty-nine-inch vertical leaps.

Bootie's system works, for him. People tell him things they don't tell the mass comm grads who do it by the book. They tell him things because they like him, and because they know he won't print about nine-tenths of what he knows.

"Willie!" Bootie says as he sets the phone down hard enough to make it ring. "How the hell are you? Long time, no drink."

Yeah, we've had a few together. Like golfers, drinkers tend to gravitate toward each other, even if they don't have much else in common.

I tell him what I have in mind. Bootie's probably the least professional journalist occupying the ever-shrinking newsroom. He's been here for forty-one years, since the day he walked in fresh out of Washington and Lee. The old sports editor, another W&L man, hired him on the spot, and he never left.

Bootie does a column three times a week, most of which focuses on things that happened before many of our would-be readers were born. Wheelie and Grubby would probably give up their corner offices to get rid of Bootie Carmichael. He's the opposite of the kind of employees they want: multiplatform news gatherers who work like dogs for peanuts because they don't know any better. They, like everyone else in Richmond, know Bootie's sometimes on the take.

But Bootie is popular, especially among our ever-diminishing Baby Boomer readers who can relate to a column about Secretariat or Pete Rose, two of Bootie's favorite causes. At least twice a year, our readers are reminded that Secretariat is the greatest horse that ever lived (he has a point) and Pete Rose was unjustly railroaded by baseball (bullshit). Every time they do a readership survey, Bootie comes out as more popular than any hard-hitting reporter or thoughtful news-side columnist we have. So, while perfectly good journalists are sent packing in the latest layoff, Bootie survives.

They've tried to make him quit on his own. He doesn't get to spend a week in Louisville drinking bourbon before the Kentucky Derby any more, and he doesn't get to go to the World Series and play poker with his cronies who also are too popular to fire. Like for most of us, raises are only a fond memory to Bootie, and he has to occasionally write what his bosses want him to write. No one can forget his epic of cluelessness on the X Games two summers ago.

He still carries the title of sports editor, but they hired a thirty-five-year-old with a future instead of a past and gave him the title of executive sports editor, which means he runs things. Everybody but Bootie concedes that executive SE outranks sports editor.

But Bootie, while he wails and moans about real and imaginary slights, has no plans to quit. He's sixty-three and says he wants to do this until he's eighty. Sally, Jackson, I and a few other old-timers have a pool on who'll go first, Wheelie, Grubby or Bootie. My money's on Bootie sitting fat and comfortable in his comfy chair eating the stale cake they'll serve at Wheelie's and Grubby's going-away parties.

I start to lay out my proposal to Bootie.

"Have you heard the latest?" he asks, interrupting. "About the company cars?"

Yes, I've heard. This one did kind of defy belief. They've sold the company cars. This was no hardship to me, since I'd rather rent a bicycle than drive most of our rolling stock. The rumor is that our latest fleet was bought from some wholesaler who got them cheap after they were flooded during Hurricane Irene. They ride, and break down, like they were sitting in salt water for a few days.

It is scary, though. If I owned stock in this fine media empire and heard that news, I think I'd be giving my broker a call.

"How the hell are we supposed to cover games in Blacksburg and down in Chapel Hill?" Bootie wails. The man is 260 pounds of pink and righteous indignation. "They kept two cars, two of the Sonatas, I think, for Grubby and the big cheeses."

I commiserate with Bootie and then steer him back to the proposal. Bootie wasn't here in 1964, but he's old-school enough to realize that there might be some merit in my idea.

In general, I don't like the long-winded tree killers that upper management used to be so fond of before a diminishing herd of reporters and the cost of newsprint made the bottom-line guys rethink the whole five-part series thing, our epic on the city's riverfront notwithstanding.

This time, though, I've made an exception. For one thing, I love baseball. For another, I'd like to do something that would make the people living around Les Hacker aware that he once was something more than an old fart who's dropping brain cells faster than I'm losing hair. Like Bootie, I can be driven by my own interests.

"It's a buffet," Sally Velez observed right after the last cuts. "Serve yourself."

"The '64 Vees, huh?" Bootie says, when I bring him back around to the purpose of my visit to Toyland. "Huh. That might be interesting."

It's quid pro quo. If I can tap into the sports department's budget for a little travel money, sports can get something that might win them the national awards the executive sports editor covets. It shouldn't be too hard for Bootie to sell the ESE on that. I don't flatter myself when I tell you that whatever I write will be above the usual standards of our sports department.

"I'll take care of it," he says, winking at me in a way that lets me know it won't be aboveboard. What a surprise. Bootie once bought a jacket in Baltimore when it turned suddenly and unseasonably cold at The Preakness. When the bean counters rejected it on his expense account, he didn't argue. Instead, he turned in another expense account, complete with receipts for meals and lodging, whose bottom line was equal to the penny to the one he'd turned in originally.

"Let the sons of bitches find the jacket," he famously told our managing editor.

My idea is pretty simple, like most good ideas. I'll do a story on the 1964 Richmond Virginians, then and now. It'll be full of interviews with the old guys who are still upright, lots of memory lane crap for our core audience. It'll give what few under-forty readers we have a glimpse at what the world was like before free agency made multimillionaires out of utility infielders. (Not that I don't usually side with the multimillionaires with bats and gloves over the billionaires who arm-twist ragtag cities into building new stadiums instead of schools. But for Christ's sake, couldn't you spare a few nickels for the fans?)

I can do a lot of it in my spare time and take vacation days, if Wheelie won't swing for a paid sabbatical. Yeah, I'd be working for free. The suits love that. But sometimes, it's the only way.

Once, back when Bob Parks was city editor, I was railing about what I considered an injustice: We were only given 3 percent raises because corporate had decided we didn't turn a big enough profit.

"That's it," I said after I'd stormed into Parks's office. "From now on, I work to the contract. Forty hours and not a minute more."

Parks laughed.

"Bull."

I asked why he thought it was bull.

"Willie," he said, "do you really want to look back, at the end of the day, and say, 'I showed them. I didn't do one damn thing more than I had to. They didn't get anything extra out of me.'?"

Parks was right. Sometimes, as Sally says, you have to serve yourself.

I will need a handful of days to travel to exotic places like Tete de Fromage, Wisconsin, and East Bumfuck, Georgia, to get the "now" part right, but it won't be that hard. If I have to take vacation time to do it, hell, I usually spend my vacations at Penny Lane, anyhow.

I wander through the newsroom, killing a little time before I take Peggy over to see Les. Sarah Goodnight is standing by Mark Baer's desk, and her smile makes me wonder if, God help her, they're dating again.

"Hey, Willie," she says. "How's Les?"

I give her the company line and ask her if anything new and terrible has happened since Sunday morning.

"Oh, the usual. Chuck Apple had a meltdown. I guess you heard about the company cars."

It turns out that Chuck's ancient Toyota died about three months ago, and Chuck's been using company cars for his main source of transportation.

"He lives about five miles from here," Baer says. "He says that now he's going to have to break down and buy something."

I think about the depth of poverty that would force a person to depend on our chariots for transportation. Maybe we should take up a collection for Chuck.

I put in a call to Peachy Love. She tells me that they're waiting for Finlay Rand to return from vacation. They don't have any record of a shooting like that happening around here, or anywhere in Virginia, for the past five years at least.

"The guy must have been a nut," Peachy offers. "I mean, they've been talking to everybody, trying to find out who might have a bone to pick with your stepdaddy, and they've got nothing."

"They're not married."

"What?"

"My mother and Les. They're not married."

"OK. Guess I knew that. Still, he's like a daddy to you, right?"

I concede that he's about as close to one as I've had.

I could have told them Les doesn't have any enemies. Hell, I did tell the detective who talked to me the day after it happened. I guess they hear that a lot. "He didn't have an enemy in the world. He was the sweetest, kindest man you'd ever want to meet." In Les's case, though, it's pretty much true.

"Well," I tell Peachy, "Rand ought to be back on Wednesday. Maybe he'll know something."

A minute after I put the cell phone back in my pocket, it rings.

I'm greeted by the slightly giddy voice of Andy Peroni.

"How soon can you be ready to go to Baltimore?"

I'm quiet for a few seconds.

"Baltimore," Peroni says again. "The azaleas are blooming, the Birds are in town for an afternoon game. Time for a road trip."

I heard laughter in the background. I recognize R. P. McGonnigal.

"We decided to have a mental-health day," Peroni says. It's easy enough for Peroni to do that, since he now owns the hardware store his old man left him. And I guess McGonnigal works in a business where you aren't hanging somebody out to dry if you take a vacation day on ten minutes' notice.

I tell them I have to get Peggy and take her to the hospital.

"Then go get her," McGonnigal says, grabbing the phone. "We got four seats down the third-base line on StubHub. Hell, man, you don't even work on Mondays. You've got no excuse whatsoever."

They're right. I can drop Peggy off and get Custalow to pick her up later. Custalow hates baseball, and he really does have to work today.

We agree that they'll pick me up on Broad Street, outside the hospital, in an hour.

"Road trip!" Peroni yells. There's something in all this of the forced gaiety of men our age trying to relive what can only be lived once. No doubt there will be an ice chest full of Miller pony bottles, and Andy will be blasting beach music all the way there. I only hope he doesn't give over completely to the dream and take the convertible. It's a nice day outside, for early April, but it's not that nice.

Still, it's spring and it's baseball. I'm sure Les will understand. He'll probably want to go with us. I wish he could.

"Wait," I say just as Peroni is ringing off. "You said four tickets."

"My sister," Andy says. "She's a baseball nut, too."

I vaguely remember Andy's sister, Cindy. She was six years behind us in school. I heard she'd gotten divorced.

"Don't worry, Willie," R. P. yells into the phone. "You won't get cooties."

I DROP Peggy off. Custalow will come get her about four thirty.

I've been standing outside about ten minutes when Andy pulls to the curb. He and R. P. are in the front. I get in the back. Thank God, he took the sedan.

"Hey there, Willie Black. Am I old enough to play now?"

I haven't seen Cindy Peroni in ten years. I knew through Andy that she'd moved back to Richmond after the split and was living somewhere off Patterson in the West End.

I don't get the allusion at first. Then I remember little Cindy Peroni, her face red as a fire engine, demanding that we let her play basketball with us. She must have been in the fifth grade, and she was growing into a pretty good athlete—made all district when she was a senior, I think—but we were a bunch of knuckleheads who wanted no part of a girl in our game. It happened more than once, I'm remembering now.

Yeah, I tell Cindy. I think you're old enough now.

She's grown into her age pretty well. She still has those brown, sparkly eyes that made her a real knockout by the time she finished high school. Her hair's still brown, although whether by nature or science I can't say. She's wearing jeans and a long-sleeved Cal Ripken T-shirt, and she's wearing them well. She's either taken care of herself well or she's decided the best revenge on her former husband is to turn into a major MILF.

I ask her how long she's been back in Richmond.

"About two years," she says. "I can't believe I haven't run into you before now."

With Andy's speakers blasting out songs older than we are and he and R. P. chatting away in the front seat, Cindy and I help ourselves to a couple of pony bottles each on the way to Balmer and catch up. She's spent most of her adult life following the guy she married right after high school from Richmond to Raleigh to Charlotte to Northern Virginia while he got rich replacing woods with suburbs. She has a twenty-year-old son living up in Fairfax. She's taking courses at VCU. Her midlife crisis, God help her, seems to involve getting a degree in English.

"I got tired of his shit," is the way she delicately explains the termination of marital bliss. I'd heard from Andy that Donnie Marshman had not been the ideal husband, and that his sister had kicked Marshman out on at least one occasion for doing the horizontal hula with another party. Well, with three divorces to my credit, who am I to judge?

"I gave him back his name," Cindy says, "and he gave me a house and sends me a nice check every month."

Well, I say, it's always better to dump a rich guy than a poor one.

"True dat," she says, clinking bottles with me.

WE'VE DRIVEN around a perfectly good major-league baseball stadium to get here. Washington fans have their own team now. People are rolling around on the ground and speaking in tongues over the Nats, but our drive down memory lane doesn't go into DC.

"I'm an AL East kind of gal," Cindy says, and then proceeds to do a fifteen-minute running commentary on the Orioles' past, present and future. The Ripken T-shirt is probably older than her son, and I see that it's autographed, although Cal's signature has faded a bit.

"You ought to see my tattoo," she says.

"I probably should," I say.

"Maybe later," she says.

WE HAVE a couple more beers in one of those places outside the stadium that they must hose down after every home game, then treat ourselves to barbecue at Boog Powell's place. R. J. says it's a shame they didn't pay baseball players more when Boog was in his prime. He might not have had to sell barbecue for a living. I tell him to think about that the next time he bursts a blood vessel over some forty-year-old left-handed reliever getting a couple of million.

"Gotta be some middle ground," he mutters.

We've somehow nabbed seats twenty rows up and maybe fifty feet back of third base. We drink Natty Bohs even though I'm not that crazy about them any more, because that's what you do in Charm City. It must be seventy-five degrees. It'll probably be forty again tomorrow, but carpe the damn diem.

I yield to nature in the middle of the third inning. On my way back to our seats, I run into Cindy, coming back from a similar urge.

Just before we step into the concourse leading back to our seats, she spins me around and lands a big one right on my lips. She has to bend my head down a little and stand on tiptoes to do it. A couple of kids walking by telling us to get a room.

"Thanks," Cindy Peroni says. "I've waited to do that since I was eight years old."

I am never sure what drives human beings to bond with each other. Looking at Cindy's fine butt as she leads the way to our row, I'm just glad it works out that way sometimes.

It's a good day all around. In the seventh inning, Luke Scott hits a foul pop-up down the third-base line. Looking up into that perfect blue sky, I'm reminded of what it felt like at ten, trying to get a bead on a black dot of a ball, still learning how to be where it landed, when it landed. Usually, they look like they're coming right to you and then wind up ten rows away. This one, though, never swerved. I can never understand how those guys catch foul balls, even home-run balls, with their bare hands, and I'd never try. But this one hits two seats over, does a carom underneath the seats as we all stand, mouths open at this rare occurrence. Like I'm wearing a ball magnet, it rolls right up to my left shoe. All I have to do is pick it up. Somehow, this is cause for applause and congratulations in the general vicinity.

I give the ball to Cindy, who tells me to give it to the five-year-old girl in the row in front of us, and I tell her that's a fine idea.

The Orioles beat the Blue Jays, and I've managed to walk that tightrope between pleasantly high and stupid. At ballpark prices, I can't drink enough beer to get drunk, even with the head start I had.

On the way back to the car, I ask Cindy if she'd like to have dinner or something sometime.

"I dunno," she says, "I'm think I'm busy that night."

She pauses about two beats and then laughs.

"What the hell do you think?"

My hearing's not that great. I'll have to be stone deaf to get a hearing aid unless they can make them a lot better than they do now, but I am missing some things.

Like my cell phone. If it rings and I'm in anything except a quiet room, I don't hear it. On the way to the car, I check and see that I have two calls.

The first one is from Sally Velez.

"Hey, I thought you'd like to know," she says. "They've caught the guy."

"That shot Les?"

"Yeah. They have video surveillance in your building, outside the basement doors, where they make deliveries. Did you know that?"

No, I tell her, I didn't. Abe has never mentioned it. It makes sense, I guess. We're only an improperly closed door away from the drug dealers across Grace Street, just around the corner from the occasional chaos of Monroe Park. They must've decided to do that at a board meeting I didn't attend, which would be all of them.

"So, when the cops get around to looking at the tapes, they see this asshole with what looks like a really bad blond rug and a plaid sports jacket, coming out the alley entrance. They didn't have to look too far to find him."

An undercover cop had been hanging out in the park the last two days. Today, the sports jacket showed up, worn by a man who apparently had seen a bit more than his mind could handle on one of his many all-expenses-paid trips to Sandland, compliments of the US Army.

"His name's Raymond Gatewood," Sally says. "Four tours in Iraq, one in Afghanistan. He's been in and out of the park for the last two years. Apparently just went nuts. They said they had to Tase him twice to subdue him."

I ask Sally how he got into the building and how he laid hands on the Winchester .30-30.

"They just brought him in," she says. "One thing at a time. The cops are feeling pretty good that they caught the guy."

I check the other call, the one I should have taken first.

"Willie," my mother says, "Les isn't doing so well."

A breeze blowing in off the harbor puts a chill on my perfect afternoon.

Chapter Six

TUESDAY

Sometime yesterday afternoon, Les apparently had a stroke. He is, indeed, not doing well. Peggy's beating herself up for not being there. She had just left to go back home and catch up on some much-needed cleaning. By the time she got a ride back with Andi at five, the damage seemingly had been done. One of the nurses said he was the way he is now when they checked in on him.

When I got back last night, I wondered out loud how a man could have a stroke in a major teaching hospital and no one notices. Nobody really had a good answer for that one, although the night crew seemed pissed off that I'd had the temerity to ask.

Les's mouth is drawn to one side, and he can't seem to do much with his right arm and right leg. He looks at me like a dog that's been hit by a truck.

Today, I can't help but think about something he once told me. I'd gone with him to visit one of his old friends from his days as a roofer. The guy was in about the same shape Les is in now.

Les tried to jolly him up a bit. We left after maybe the longest half hour I could remember.

Neither of us said anything until we were back in the car. As I was turning the ignition key, Les said, "Willie, if I ever get like that, please shoot me."

CINDY COMES by for a while. She and Peggy remember each other from the old days on the Hill.

None of us feel much like talking. At one point, I look over and Peggy's holding one of his hands while Awesome Dude holds the other one.

Somehow, Jimmy Deacon gets word about Les's turn for the worse. Jumpin' Jimmy is subdued, for him. But he's still doing his best to get Les to smile, which I'm not sure is possible right now.

"Openin' Day, man," Jimmy says, clapping his hands and startling the nurses. "Just two days until they throw out the first pitch. Gimme some peanuts and Cracker Jacks!"

Les just lies there, looking straight ahead. He's managed to cheer us up so much over the years, often just by being Les, and now we can't seem to do a damn thing to return the favor.

When I've had about all I can bear without crying, I step out into the hall, headed for somewhere that allows smoking. Jumpin' Jimmy joins me.

"Geez," Jimmy says, "that's tough. But old Les'll pull through. You can bet your bottom damn dollar on that."

But he kind of chokes up when he says it. Even Jumpin' Jimmy Deacon is having trouble whistling a happy tune today.

"You know," he says, changing the subject, "you asked me about Frannie Fling."

I have to think for a couple of seconds before I make the connection.

"Well," he says, "today's April 10. That was the day it happened. I don't forget dates or players."

I'm fishing for a cigarette.

"What? What happened on April 10?"

"April 10, 1965. That was the day she did it."

I ask him to be a little less cryptic. I'm already switching from concerned human being to journalist, taking mental notes for my big piece on the '64 Vees, homing in on some local color.

"She went down to Florida that spring. I guess she thought she could get Whitestone to do right by her."

I ask Jimmy if he would mind starting at the beginning, or at least at some point where I can catch up.

Frannie Fling was, Jimmy says, a Baseball Annie. She liked baseball players. She liked them a lot, and she wanted them to like her, too.

"She was a runaway, from up north somewhere. New Hampshire, I think. No, wait, Vermont. Yeah, Wells, Vermont." He taps his addled head. "I never forget stuff from the past. It's the present that's a bitch sometimes."

Jimmy tells me he thinks Frannie Fling was eighteen in 1964. She showed up at Parker Field one day in February, looking for a job.

"I think she'd been a waitress or something before that," Jimmy says. "Anyhow, the GM hired her, probably because she was pretty. She had these bedroom eyes that just sparkled, and kind of devilish-lookin' eyebrows. Brown hair. Built like a brick shithouse—excuse me for being crude, but she was. She looked like she was ready for just about anything. Maybe it wasn't such a good thing that she got that job with the Vees."

Jimmy says they employed her to sell concessions, work in the ticket office and do whatever else needed doing.

"They even had her wear that mascot outfit. She would do anything they asked her. Hell, she'd work with me getting the field ready."

When the players came north from Florida, it didn't take them long to start sniffing around Frances Flynn.

"I tried to kind of warn her," Jimmy says. "I tried to tell her those boys weren't into buying anything at that point in their lives. They was more into short-term rentals, if you know what I mean."

She wasn't a bad person, Jimmy said, but she was young and not inclined to listen to the advice of a jackleg minor-league baseball gofer like him. She told him she had been an honors student in high school, but that she just woke up one day and realized she was going to spend the rest of her life living and working in this little Vermont town. And so she left, halfway through her senior year of high school.

"She said she wanted to go somewhere where it didn't snow in April."

She had meant to go all the way to Florida, but she had a friend who had enrolled at Richmond Professional Institute and had a spare bed. After waiting tables and figuring that was about as glamorous in Richmond as it was in Wells, Vermont, she saw an ad in the paper one day advertising for a "position" with the Richmond Vees.

"She said she had always liked baseball, and when she found out the Vees were the Yankees' Triple-A team, her being a Yankees fan her whole life, she was like, 'How could I say no?'"

It was, I suppose, something of a rush to have young studs, maybe guys who would be playing in Yankee Stadium someday soon, tripping over their dicks to be near you. At any rate, Frances Flynn was soon Frannie Fling.

"She started with Phil Holt," Jimmy says. "He had a fiancée back in Alabama, but Alabama was a long way from Richmond. Holt was in a two-bedroom apartment with three other guys, and it wasn't exactly a secret that Frannie was doin' the nasty with him."

Jumpin' Jimmy knows for sure, or at least on second-hand knowledge, that she slept with Jack Velasquez, Roy Haas, Rip Rittenbacker and Rabbit Larue.

"She might of done the whole team," Jimmy says. "They was always joking that Frannie had batted around."

Jimmy holds up his right hand like a traffic cop at an intersection.

"Wait! Scratch that. The one she didn't sleep with, that I'm sure she didn't sleep with, was Les. Well, him and Buck McRae. Buck was black, and it was, you know, 1964."

I don't bother telling Jumpin' Jimmy about my dad, the late Artie Lee, or why my mother named me Willie Mays Black.

My African-American heritage would just get in the way of Jimmy's story, and the best thing a good reporter can do is not get in the way.

Before I can ask him what was wrong with Les, he answers the question.

"Les wasn't like that. Les was already married. He was a little older than some of the other fellas, and maybe he was just more decent. Anyhow, when they'd start laughing about ol' Frannie Fling, he'd just move away or tell them to act their ages.

"One time, I heard him ask Holt, who'd managed to take pictures of Frannie the night before, buck naked, how he'd feel if that was his sister.

"Holt just stared at him like he was crazy. He said, 'My sister wouldn't do shit like that.' They all respected Les, mostly because he could have kicked most if not all their asses, but you could tell the Frannie Fling thing kind of drove a ledge between him and the other boys."

I'm sure Jimmy means "wedge," but I'm not about to interrupt now.

"I wondered if all the shit that summer, and what happened in Florida next spring, wasn't the last straw that broke the camel's back for Les. I mean, he kind of knew his day had come and gone, but it seemed like the fun had gone out of it for him. The Vees had up and left for Toledo, but Les came back to Richmond that spring. He was done with baseball."

"But about Frannie Fling . . ."

"Oh, yeah. Well, by July, she had worked around to Whitestone. Which was bad news."

Lucky Whitestone, I already know from my research and what Bootie Carmichael has told me secondhand, was the Chosen One on the Vees that year.

"They thought he was goin' to be the next Yankee superstar," Jimmy says. "And he might have been, if he hadn't screwed up and got himself traded to Cleveland for a pitcher with a dead arm and an outfielder that couldn't hit left-handers.

He developed some bad habits, the way guys do who have too much looks and talent and time on their hands. But he still had a pretty damn good career. Ten years in the bigs. Lifetime batting average was .278. Not bad for a shortstop."

When Frannie and Whitestone hooked up, the rest of the team kind of backed off. There was a pecking order, as there always is, whether you're a lawyer or a left fielder, and Lucky Whitestone was at the top of it.

Many of his teammates, Jimmy says, were surprised that a guy leading the International League in batting and slugging percentage while playing an above-average game at shortstop would cast his lot with someone who'd already slept with several of his teammates.

"But Frannie was something. I swear to God she could of been a movie star, if she'd of gone in that direction. She could charm the pants off you."

Obviously, I observe.

"Whitestone had this orange GTO convertible, and they'd come driving up to the park together, waving at everybody like they were celebrities. He'd been able, with his signing bonus I guess, to afford more than the other boys, so he had his own apartment, which gave 'em a little bit of privacy. But the GM wasn't happy about it, and one day the Yankees sent some suit down to give him a talking to. It wasn't what future Yankees did, the suit told him. Whitestone told the guy to go fuck himself. Or at least, that's what he told everybody he said."

Lucky Whitestone hit .317 for the Vees that year, with twenty home runs. When the IL season ended in late August, he was called up to the Yankees. He was twenty-three years old, and his future seemed as safe as General Motors stock.

Jimmy throws down his smoked-out butt and stomps on it.

"I doubt if Whitestone knew, when he left, that she was pregnant."

Jimmy says he figures he was the first one connected with the ball club to know. When the 1964 season ended, so did Frannie Fling's employment with the Vees, because their scumbag carpetbagging owner moved them to Toledo, Ohio, and left us without a team in 1965. Also, the general manager who'd hired her was now convinced that she was a bad influence on the players. So, she was back to waiting tables.

"I went around to see her, must have been late September, to see how she was doin'. Her friend who was at RPI had dropped out, and Frannie was sharing a place with two girls she didn't hardly know. I could tell something was wrong, and I finally got her to tell me.

"I talked her into writing Whitestone about it, because I thought, you know, he might want to do right by her."

Instead, Jimmy says, she told him later she wrote him three times and finally got his phone number and called him, at his home down in Florida. He told her they'd do "something about it" in the spring, that she had to give him some time to get his act together, straighten things out with an old girlfriend back home, or some such bullshit.

"I didn't do enough for her," Jimmy says. "Nobody did.

"And then, she went back to Vermont, right dead in the middle of winter. I don't think she had much choice. The other two girls left, and she couldn't pay the rent.

"I offered to let her stay at my place. Hell, I could of slept on the couch. But she said no, Lucky wouldn't like that. Like he gave a shit."

It was early March when Jimmy heard from her again. She called from the Greyhound station, on her way from Vermont to Florida. Lucky Whitestone had sent her money for a bus ticket, she said. Almost as an aside, she told Jimmy that her parents had kicked her out when they saw she was pregnant, and that she had spent the last couple of months bunking in a friend's folks' house.

She told Jimmy it wouldn't be a big wedding, that Lucky didn't want anything big that would detract from his efforts to become a full-fledged New York Yankee, but that he'd broken off with his now former girlfriend back home.

"She must of been at least six, maybe seven months along by then," Jimmy says. "I offered to pick her up at the bus station and buy her a decent meal, even drive her down to Florida. I had a lot of energy back then."

Watching Jimmy hop from one foot to the other, unable to hold still for two seconds, I can only imagine.

"But she said, no, the bus for Miami was leaving in fifteen minutes, she just wanted to say hi, and that she'd be drinking fresh-squeezed orange juice for breakfast. But she sounded tired."

Jimmy sighs.

"That's the last I heard from her."

He found out most of what happened secondhand. He'd gotten to know the Vees, who were now the Toledo Mud Hens. He called Rabbit Larue one day while the team was still in Florida, just to say hi.

They talked a little bit, and then Larue asked him if he heard about Frannie Fling. He said he hadn't, that she'd called on her way down to Florida to get married.

Larue seemed to think that was funny. And then he told Jimmy what Lucky Whitestone did.

Larue said he was surprised Frannie hadn't shown up with the cops, and that he bet "Lucky hasn't heard the last of her."

Whitestone had been surprised to see her.

"Which made me think that maybe Frannie was maybe paintin' a little brighter picture than it really was," Jimmy says. "Maybe gildin' the lily a little bit."

They way Jimmy heard it, Whitestone said she came to his room at the motel the next morning after she called from Richmond and said they had to get married. He told the other players that he wasn't about to get married to "some whore like that." Whatever he said to her, she must have gotten kind of hysterical, the way you do when you're in the third trimester, your family's kicked you out and the guy who knocked you up is calling you a whore.

He told her to take it easy, that he was going to make it right, just don't call anybody. He told her he'd get her a room and then he'd come by later.

He reserved the room and got her settled and calmed down. When he called her back after the intrasquad game, his plan was in motion.

He told her he'd found a preacher who would do the ceremony right there in the hotel. There was a big ballroom, and they could have the wedding and some kind of bullshit reception right there.

Frannie had brought along something that would pass for a wedding dress in the one suitcase she had. When Whitestone came to get her, it was already seven P.M. He told her it was OK, that night weddings were kind of special. Larue told Jimmy that Whitestone had even borrowed a tux to set up the gag just right.

So, when they came into the ballroom, the only other person Frannie sees is the preacher. When she looks closer, she sees that it's actually the Vees' third-base coach. Whitestone assures her that he is certified to do weddings in the state of Florida.

She asked her husband-to-be, as they're walking toward the minister, if he has a best man.

"Oh," Lucky Whitestone is supposed to have said, "I've got plenty of them."

And that's when the curtain that divided the room into two parts opened, and out came most of the rest of the Richmond Vees' starting lineup from the year before.

He told Frannie he'd decided that, since they couldn't figure exactly whose baby she was carrying, they decided she'd just have to marry the whole damn team. They kept her there and made her go through the whole ceremony. Larue said that, for a ring, Whitestone had rolled up a rubber and punched a hole through it. Then he handed her a one-way bus ticket to New York City and said to have fun on her honeymoon.

When she started crying, he apparently explained to her, with all his teammates encircling her, that every one of them would swear that she had willingly screwed them, and that if she knew what was good for her, she'd get the hell out of there before they gave her a wedding night she'd never forget.

She returned to her room, and when Lucky asked at the front desk in the morning, the clerk said she'd already checked out. Larue said he was kind of nervous the next couple of days, but he never heard from Frannie Fling again.

After Larue told Jumpin' Jimmy the story, Jimmy tried to get in touch with her. She'd shown him a letter her parents sent her the season before, with a return address in that Vermont town. Whoever answered when he called hung up on Jimmy when he told them who he was looking for.

"I didn't find out what happened to her until sometime in mid-April, I guess," Jimmy says. "I was hanging out at the ballpark, just because that's what you do in April. This fella who had been the assistant GM the year before, looking for a job anywhere he could get one, was there, too, and he told me what happened to Frannie."

They found her in a motel room in Oak Ridge, Tenn. Nobody has a clue how she got there. She had slit her wrists on the tenth, and the maid didn't find her body until the next day. The baby was dead, too, of course. It took them two days after that to get in touch with her parents, and it took the parents about three days to sic the lawyers on Lucky Whitestone. She'd sent her parents a letter, telling them that she and Whitestone were going to be married. They didn't know a lot about what their disowned daughter had been up to, but they knew enough to sue.

"Too bad they didn't give more of a shit when she was alive," Jimmy says.

If Whitestone hadn't been a top prospect, it might have ended differently. But the Yankees dug into their deep pockets and turned a battery of New York lawyers loose on Frances Flynn's reputation. Lots of guys were willing to testify to her sexual dalliances. There were threats of a countersuit. In the end, the family settled for an amount that was less than Lucky Whitestone's first-year major-league salary, just to bury their daughter with a little dignity.

"They didn't care nothin' about Whitestone," Jimmy says, "but they didn't want anything besmirking the fine Yankee tradition. Hell, after the family settled, they traded his ass to Cleveland.

"I visited her grave up there one time," Jimmy says.

"In Vermont?"

"Yeah. Had a hell of a time findin' it. The family had moved on, to Massachusetts or somewhere like that. Somebody told me that her father died and her mother sold the house the next year. She might have had other family, but I didn't stick around long enough to find out."

"What did you do? I mean, did you leave flowers or something?"

Jimmy doesn't answer for a beat or two.

"Yeah. Left some flowers. I remember one time she said she liked yellow roses, so I got some. Her grave was way up some hill. Didn't see any other Flynns around it."

I observe that it seems like he went a long way to pay respects to someone he hardly knew.

"Well," Jimmy says, "she was nice, you know? She might of had a screw or two loose, but she was a good-hearted girl, and she deserved better than what she got."

I'm thinking Jimmy might have been a little in love with Frannie Fling himself. She could have done, and did do, worse.

CINDY OFFERS to give Peggy a ride home later. I don't think my mother's planning to spend any long periods of time away from the hospital, just long enough to make sure the house is still standing. Awesome Dude's already left. I guess he's perambulating somewhere between the hospital and Oregon Hill.

I almost forgot I have a meeting with Grubby at two. It's five after by the time I get there. Sandy McCool ushers me in.

I asked Wheelie about getting a short sabbatical to do the story on the 1964 Vees, but it turns out managing editors don't have the authority, or balls, to approve such a major undertaking. He said I'd have to ask Grubby.

James H. Grubbs, former boy reporter and present publisher, looks as good as ever, which means "not very." I don't know if sunlight bounces off his skin or if he just never goes outside, but he is about the same shade as the copy paper on his desk, and he looks as if a good breeze would blow him away. He's working his iPhone when I walk in, and he doesn't stop, barely bothers to look up.

"Five minutes late," he says by way of greeting.

"I hope I'm not interrupting anything."

"Oh," he says, "don't worry. I'd never let you interrupt anything."

"After all I've done for you."

He emits a sound that would be a laugh, were it accompanied by any show of merriment whatsoever.

"Like give me gray hair and ulcers?"

I figure it's a fool's errand to mention that I've also given him some damn good stories when they were in short supply in our ever-shrinking newsroom. It's an even bigger fool's errand to mention that selling his soul to the devil probably gave him his gray hair and ulcers.

So I cut to the chase. I explain, in as few words as possible, about my idea for a takeout on the 1964 Vees, our last Yankees farm team.

"We have a sports department," Grubby notes.

"Bootie says it's fine with him."

Grubby does actually laugh at that one.

"Everything's fine with Bootie. Did you bring him some Scotch?"

I mention that our sports guys don't have time to go to the bathroom anymore. One guy's covering the whole prep beat and another one's responsible for two major college athletic programs plus auto racing.

"And you do? You've got plenty of time?"

I say the only thing I can think of.

"I'll make it worth your while."

When I mention the Frannie Fling angle, he seems slightly more interested. He can see that there might be a hook.

"Yeah," he says. "You might be able to get some of the old geezers to talk about that. That'd be interesting."

I mention that my mother's "special friend" was on the team.

"Ah," Grubby says. "So you've got an angle. Well, maybe he can tell you some inside stuff."

I tell him that Les is in the hospital, recovering from a gunshot wound and a stroke. It was in the paper, I remind him.

"Oh yeah," Grubby says, as he uses the little stylus to respond to someone in the ether who must be more important than me. "Sorry. I hope he's OK."

I'm sure you do, I think.

"Well," he says, looking up "how much sabbatical do you need?"

"A month." I try not to make it sound like a question.

"A week," he replies.

I try to get him to settle for two, but he won't budge. Hell, if it takes more than a week, I'll use vacation time. And I've got about six unpaid furlough days waiting to be wasted.

We both say OK, and then he doesn't say anything else, which is my cue to exit.

I blow Sandy McCool a kiss on the way out and tell her to get Grubby a sunlamp.

I'm playing Internet solitaire at my desk when my roomie Abe Custalow calls.

"Just wanted you to know," he says. "Rand is back."

Finlay Rand apparently returned from his vacation this afternoon to find his apartment more or less trashed, as much by the cops as by the shooter. That'll teach him to leave a contact number with somebody before he leaves town.

The police have already been by to play Twenty Questions with him.

"He's not too happy," Custalow says. "He says the guy who broke in damaged a couple of old chairs he said were worth $5,000 each. Can a chair be worth that much, Willie?"

"I don't know. Does it have beer-can holders on the arms?"

"Anyhow, he said he'd like to talk to you."

"Why?" I can't think of much that Finlay Rand and I have in common. He's a fine-wine kind of guy, and the only kind of Burgundy I've drunk much of is the hearty kind, Chateau Gallo.

"I guess about the shooting. He knows Les lives with Peggy. Maybe he wants to apologize for not putting a better lock on his door."

I remind Custalow that Gillespie has told me Rand's place was entered with a key. No muss, no fuss.

I tell Abe I'll call on Mr. Rand tomorrow, which will be the first day of my poorly funded sabbatical.

IT'S A zero-sum game in the newsroom these days. If somebody takes a week or two off, somebody else has to double up. No cushion anymore. And if the beat is night cops and it's starting to get warm on the poor side of town, you can't just blow it off. People die, and other people want to know about it. Everybody bitches about all the bad news in the paper, but try making a living printing stories about people doing the right thing. The right thing's boring to Bubba and Mary Catherine sitting on their West End screened-in porch. Reading about the down and dirty is what gets people's juices flowing. Shouldn't be that way, but Les Hacker shouldn't be in VCU hospital paralyzed on his right side. Shouldn't doesn't mean a damn thing.

So, I'm pretty sure Sarah Goodnight's not being sincere when she stops in front of my desk and says, "Thanks a lot."

Because she's been to a dirt nap or two, she gets to be me the next week or so. Wheelie probably expects her to keep covering city council, too. "Excuse me, Mayor. Could you hold off voting on that new sanitation dump for an hour or so? Somebody just caught some lead in the East End."

Sarah's a good newshound. As soon as one of our time-worn political reporters dies or retires (which, from the look of them, won't be too long now), she'll be covering state politics. Unlike me, she probably won't screw it up and wind up doing a repeat performance as night police reporter.

I apologize for the inconvenience and promise to buy her a few rounds when I get back.

"You better," she says.

I tell her I'll probably be around most of the time. Two or three trips to exotic places like Wisconsin and north Florida ought to be the extent of my travels. Plus, I don't want to be away from Les and Peggy for too long.

It's a quiet night. I go to the microfilm and do a little research on the '64 Vees.

Then, about nine, Kate calls. I tell her I mailed the rent check on the fifth, which is almost true. She interrupts me.

"What do you know about Raymond Gatewood?"

I tell her I know he should rot in hell. I fill her in on the latest on Les.

"Oh, God. I'm so sorry. Shit. This makes it even more awkward."

"What?"

There's a pause.

"I'm probably going to be his lawyer. One of them at least."

It doesn't compute for a few seconds.

"You're going to defend the guy who tried to kill Les?"

"Everybody deserves a lawyer, Willie."

I should have seen it coming. She's working with Marcus Green now, and he's a magnet for cases like Raymond Gatewood's. After getting pulled into a couple of hopeless causes that turned out to be not so hopeless after all, thanks to a little help from yours truly, my ex-wife decided that teaming up with a self-promoting, muckraking defender of truth, justice and the American way was more fun than the corporate tedium of Bartley, Bowman and Bush.

I just hope that Mr. Ellis is bringing in steady income. Hell, they're a two-lawyer family. Not to worry, even with a baby on the way.

I tell Kate that some people don't deserve shit.

"I know how you feel, but you should see this guy, Willie. I'm not sure he could find the elevator to the ninth floor, let alone get his hands on a rifle and hit something—somebody—halfway across Monroe Park."

I tell her it isn't too damn hard to lay hands on a gun in Virginia. It's probably harder to buy a pack of cigarettes.

"I know. I know. But he just seems so, I don't know, helpless."

"Les Hacker is helpless. I've seen helpless today."

She sighs.

"I'm sorry, Willie. I really am. I just wanted you to know. Somebody's got to make sure he really did do it."

I tell her that's what the police are for.

Kate Ellis, the former Kate Black, is always going to take on the hopeless case. She even took me on for longer than she should have.

I have the grace to ask her how the baby's doing and when it's due.

"October. I told you."

I resist the urge to advise her that maybe she ought to take it easy for a while. Kate has never taken it easy.

Chapter Seven

WEDNESDAY

I drive Peggy over to the hospital. She asks me if I mind if she finishes her joint on the way over. Why the hell not? She probably needs some chemical support. I suggest that she might consider moving somewhere like Seattle, where her affinity for weed won't be so much of an issue. She says she doesn't like rain. Awesome Dude, riding in the back seat, helps her toke it down to what couldn't even be called a roach about the time we park. A fume of illegal smoke follows us as we leave the car.

I spend a couple of hours at the hospital, then leave Peggy and Awesome there. Les seems about the same. Some cheerful uniformed soul came in and started chirping about rehabilitation. Her optimism did not seem to convey to Les, who mostly stared up at the ceiling.

I called Finlay Rand before I left home and arranged to meet him in his unit at noon.

Rand answers and ushers me in. He's probably a little older than me but better preserved, with a salt-and-pepper mustache. What little bit of hair he has left is swept back and shouts out "sixty-dollar haircut." He must have someone else to meet today, because he's decked out in better threads than I'd wear to a funeral. I'm trying not to be self-conscious about my wear-it-'til-it-smells-bad shirt and the mustard stain on my khakis.

His unit and mine are twins of each other, but those twins must have been separated at birth.

Custalow and I have a lighted Miller sign facing the card table that works equally well for fine dining and poker parties. Finlay Rand has a table that might have belonged to one of the more affluent kings of France. Where it's set up, he could make it as long as fourteen feet, and I have no doubt he has the leaves to do it. The frame for the art above it probably is worth more than my Honda.

Our hardwood floors' scuff marks are mostly hidden by throw rugs from Target. Rand's are covered with Oriental carpets so valuable he won't serve red wine at parties. I'm surprised he doesn't ask me to take my shoes off at the door.

The thirty-foot hallway leading to Rand's living area is like an art gallery. He's had special lighting put in to showcase modern shit that, for all I know, could be hanging upside down. Our walls don't have paintings. Our walls need painting.

Rand shows me the chairs he says were "irreparably damaged."

"It looks like someone sat on this one, and the leg broke," he says. I'm imagining Gillespie plopping his fat ass down on it.

Still, Rand's a congenial soul, not stuffy or snobbish so that it shows. He does, though, seem a bit agitated.

"I wanted to ask you for something," he says. He offers me lunch, which I decline, and some (white) wine, which I don't.

"You work at the paper. I know the, ah, shooting was a big story, but it is attracting the wrong kind of attention."

I'm not sure what he's getting at, but I'm sure he'll get to it soon enough.

"I wonder," he says, taking a sip, "if it would be possible for you not to mention my name in all the following stories. With the man caught and the trial coming up . . . well, I just don't want that kind of publicity."

"Why? I mean, it's not like it reflects on you. Could've been anybody's apartment."

He sets his glass down.

"But the kind of people I deal with, Mr. Black, they expect me to be like Caesar's wife, above reproach."

I tell Rand he's so far over reproach that he couldn't see it with binoculars.

He laughs.

"I know. I know. But just seeing my name in a story about something this . . . unpleasant could have an adverse effect on what I do."

Since what he does is get rich people to pay $20,000 for the table he glommed for $5,000 at an estate sale, I get his meaning. I tell him, though, that I can't just go in and tell the managing editor we can't use someone's name.

"But I'm an innocent bystander," he says, frowning and spreading his arms for emphasis.

I tell him I'll do what I can to keep him out of the lime-light, but I'm making no promises.

He sighs and says he'd appreciate any help I could give him.

As I'm leaving, he says, "So, what do you cover for the newspaper?"

Obviously, he's not a subscriber, which puts him in the strong majority in the greater metropolitan area. I explain, and he kind of wrinkles his nose.

"Must be awful," he says. "All that blood."

Finlay Rand looks as if he might faint if he cut himself shaving. I tell him you get used to it.

He thinks to mention Les.

"I'm so sorry about the gentleman who was shot. I understand you know him?"

I explain, as delicately as possible, my link to Les Hacker.

"Well," he says, "almost like family."

"Exactly like family."

For some reason, I mention the story I'm doing on the '64 Vees.

"Ah, yes. Baseball. I never was much of a sports fan myself. I must go over to the stadium and see a game sometime."

I'm thinking right after pigs fly.

I tell him again I'll do what I can, and he sees me out.

After lunch, I get started. I Google Phil Holt and Lucky Whitestone and find out it's pretty much the way Jumpin' Jimmy remembers it.

Holt, who spent parts of five seasons with the A's, was managing a Kwik Mart in his hometown, which is what you did before free agency when your arm wore out and you hadn't bothered to go to college. He was in the store just before closing time, by himself, that night in 1985 when it happened. Somebody thought they saw a guy leaving the parking lot in a white or cream-colored car, but that's about all they had to go on. Nobody found Holt's body until sometime after two, when a cop noticed the lights were still on and investigated. Nothing I read indicated anybody was ever caught.

Lucky Whitestone's hunting accident happened three years later. He had a little more money than Holt, I guess, from playing ten years in the bigs. At least, it doesn't appear that he had been reduced to running a second-rate convenience store. He retired to Tallahassee, probably signed his old baseball cards at memorabilia shows, maybe got to be grand marshal of the Christmas parade.

At any rate, he was somewhere in the swamp or woods or whatever, deer hunting with a couple of buddies. One of them said he heard a shot and thought Lucky had bagged a buck. When the two of them got there, though, they found out that Lucky was the baggee, not bagger. As with Holt, the cops never seem to have found out what happened. There were a lot of hunters out that day, the first day of hunting season, but nobody saw anything out of the ordinary, other than one very dead ex-major leaguer with part of his head blown off.

The two guys Les remembered didn't seem to have met with foul play, either accidental or on purpose.

Jackson Rittenbacker, the home run and strikeout king, lived to the ripe old age of sixty-one, retiring to his hometown, Eau Claire, Wisconsin. He was on a motorboat out on Lake Michigan, fishing, when he disappeared. He was presumed drowned, although they never found his body.

Roy Haas did, as Les remembered, die of a heart attack in 2008. He made it to seventy, making him a Methuselah among the 1964 Richmond Vees, from my research so far. He'd been one of the stars of the '64 team, hitting over .300 with fifteen home runs, but then he hurt his knee in spring training the next year and never had more than a few September at bats in the bigs before he hung up his spikes.

In a story in the Sacramento paper, his wife said he'd had some health problems but nothing serious. Maybe he should have had a checkup or drunk more red wine.

I'm going down the opening-day starting lineup, and there are a lot of guys on the DL—Dead List. The starting pitcher, Holt, and the shortstop, third baseman and center fielder, Whitestone, Haas and Rittenbacker, all taken from us.

This isn't like trying to track down World War II vets. Two of these guys didn't make it to fifty, and the other two fell way below the average life expectancy of male human beings in the United States.

I'm starting to wonder if there's a member of the starting lineup with whom I can actually converse without conducting a séance. Only Les is above ground, and he's sure as hell in no condition to talk.

I can't find out anything much about Jack Velasquez after he retired. His full name was Joaquin Diego Velasquez, but someone probably figured he had a better chance at acceptance in the US of A if he went with "Jack."

Velasquez hit for a pretty good average and was a slick fielder, which might have worked if he'd played second or short. But he was a first baseman, and he was expected to deliver the long ball. Jack Velasquez delivered the short ball instead, hitting only five home runs in 1964. He played three more years in the minors and then went home, to a place that my US map shows is near Miami. And then, nothing.

I still have a second baseman, a right fielder and a left fielder to track down, in addition to Velasquez, but I promised Peggy I'd come by and get her, and I want to spend some more time with Les.

At the hospital, I talk with Les, but it's pretty much a monologue. When I tell him I'm going to do a story on the 1964 Vees, he shakes his head and says something that sounds like, "Long time ago."

The doctor who comes by doesn't seem too concerned, or at least not concerned enough, about how a guy who was strong as an ox, albeit a slightly addlepated one, six days ago is now drooling.

"These things happen sometimes," is about as close to expert medical advice as I can get from him without squeezing his neck. I refrain.

Andi comes around four. We're playing tag team a lot. She'll take Peggy and Awesome home later.

Awesome Dude really is rising to the occasion, as much as a guy can who's about two beers short of a six-pack. He's right at Peggy's side, and he keeps up a steady stream intended to cheer up Les. When I walk out of the room, he follows me.

"He's gonna be OK, though, right, Willie?" he asks me just outside the door.

I can't make any such promises. I just tell Awesome that Les is tough, that he can lick anything.

"Yeah," Awesome says. "He's a tough dude."

I look in the room over Awesome's shoulder, and Peggy looks at me and shakes her head. She looks like she's about as close to crying as I've ever seen her. I wish there was more I could say to either of them.

I thank Andi for coming and ask her how school's going.

"Not bad," she says. I ask her if she can tell me more.

"I think I want to go into social work," she says. "It might be nice to use my degree to help somebody, you know?"

I try not to show my dismay.

"Isn't that going to take awhile?" I ask, thinking about all those now-worthless courses in English and psychology.

She looks at me and shakes her head.

"Dad," she says, obviously exasperated that I doubt her ability to chart her academic course. "I've figured it out. I've done all my electives. I can get an undergraduate degree by the end of the next school year if I load up on degree courses."

I'm about to say how swell that is. She could finish in five years, only one more than I'd hoped for. One of my rare good deeds has been paying Andi's tuition and fees. It's weak payback for all the years I was an invisible father. When she graduates, I'll be getting a big raise.

But then I remember that there was an extra word in Andi's last sentence.

"Undergraduate?"

"Well," she says, "you really can't do much with a social work degree if you don't get a master's."

I'm about to say that you probably can't do much with a master's, either. I'm kind of glad my only offspring isn't inclined to be a money-grubbing MBA, but not being a ward of the state wouldn't be such a bad thing.

"But," she goes on, seeing me on the verge of a swoon, "I can do it in one extra year, and there's loans and all. I can help out."

I ask her if she's still going to spend half her time as a waitress.

"Dad, they call them servers now, or waitstaff. And I can cut back a little on that. Plus, Tee's got a good job."

Ah, yes. Tee. Andi's "roommate." I don't even want to know. I did make the mistake once of asking her if his parents were so poor that they could only afford one letter for his first name. She informed me that his full name, if it was any of my business, was Thomas Jefferson Blandford V. I guess they ran out of Toms and Jeffs and Trips and such. Anyhow, I'm pretty damn sure somebody with a roman numeral five after his name isn't after Andi's inheritance.

But it looks like I'm going to have to keep Grubby from firing me for another couple of years, at least.

I promise my daughter we'll make it work. At least that's more honest than promising Awesome and Peggy that Les is going to pull through.

I can hear Penny Lane whispering my name on the way home, but I'm on a mission. I have some people to find.

When I get back to the Prestwould, though, Custalow informs me that there has been "a little excitement."

It seems that Finlay Rand had an extra key. He kept it in this big-ass Chinese vase that sat in the hallway next to the elevator, between his unit and the other one on the ninth floor. He said he left it there so the cleaning lady would be able to get in when he was gone.

When he realized it was gone, he called the cops, who were mightily interested in why he'd waited so damn long to tell them about the extra key. This led to a couple of detectives conducting what was apparently a rather rigorous interview.

Feldman, our very own McGrumpy, overheard much of what was going on, partly because he was lurking on the landing below. Feldman has never been one to shy away from potential gossip.

And, when the cops finally left, McGrumpy was able to "console" Rand and, in the process, hear the whole story.

Feldman being Feldman, within half an hour two different widows from different floors of the Prestwould are calling Rand to tell him how sorry they are for his troubles.

The way Abe relayed it to me, Rand caught Feldman in the lobby and threatened to slap his toupee off if he didn't mind his own business. He was loud enough to draw the attention of Marcia the manager, who called Custalow. Unfortunately, he arrived before Rand could actually do damage to McGrumpy.

"Couldn't you have walked a little slower?" I ask Abe.

I could see the cops' point. If there was another key to Finlay Rand's apartment, somebody obviously used it to get in and shoot Les. And that somebody would have known the key was there. I'm thinking somebody is already rattling the cleaning lady's cage. But how knowledge of that key made its way to Raymond Gatewood down in Monroe Park eludes me. Of course, all of it pales in elusiveness to the mystery of why anyone would shoot the world's kindest ex-minor league catcher in the first place.

I call Kate.

"I didn't think you'd be speaking to me," she says.

I tell her that I wouldn't mind having a conversation with her client.

She seems surprised. She says she'll check with Marcus Green to see if she can set it up.

Kate wasn't born yesterday.

"Something's changed."

I tell her maybe, maybe not.

"Well, if you see fit to tell me more, it might make an interview with Gatewood possible."

"Just give me a few minutes with him," I tell her.

"Why? You're not going to hurt him, are you?"

"I just want to make sure about something."

"I thought you said that's what the cops were for."

"Touché."

So I tell her about the key.

"I wonder why he didn't tell the cops about it before," Kate says.

"If I knew that, I wouldn't be calling you."

I've barely gotten off the phone with my latest ex-wife when Rand calls.

"I need to talk with you," he says.

WHEN I get there, he's a little more pale than he was the last time I saw him. Being grilled by Richmond's finest seems to have faded some of his spa-grown tan.

"I just didn't want any more publicity," he says. He has a glass of red wine in his hand, which is shaking a little. He doesn't think to ask me if I want one. "I forgot about the other key until I realized it was Della's day to clean. I thought about not telling the police at all, because I know it's just going to bring more notoriety. But I knew that wouldn't be right."

I tell him what I've learned from covering cover-ups of one kind or another for more than half my life. Truth will out. You think you've got the bastard locked up in a steel cage, then you turn around and it's running bare-assed naked down the street for everybody to see. Politicians in particular seem incapable of learning this, but it seems to hold true for the general populace as well, even well-heeled antiques dealers.

"Now," he says, "they're going to want to talk to me again. I don't suppose there's any chance anymore of keeping my name out of the paper."

I don't tell him that the cops wouldn't give us a tip if the city was being eaten by Godzilla. They're genetically programmed to keep information from the news media and, thus, the public.

I also don't tell him that I'm about to rat him out as bad as McGrumpy did. It's a matter of priorities. Do I help a rich guy on the ninth floor who barely knows my name, or do I help the young, talented and lovely Sarah Goodnight, who could make much hay out of a tip like this, and to whom I owe at least one big favor?

No-brainer. I tell Rand I'll see what I can do, but that our reporters have very good contacts with the police. Which is true. If Custalow hadn't been plugged in to everything that goes on around here, I probably would have gotten a call from Peachy Love, who knows all and tells some.

I have a Miller or three while I continue my research, or as much of it as I can do from my antique home computer. Wonder if Rand could get anything for it?

Three hours, a lot of strikeouts and a couple of hits later, I'm sitting and staring at my computer screen.

All I can think to do is invoke our Lord and Savior's first and last names and middle initial.

"Jesus H. Christ."

Chapter Eight

Thursday

"*W*hat the hell is an Altoona Curve?"

Jimmy Deacon is only being academic, or as academic as Jumpin' Jimmy ever gets. He's been aware of the Curve for at least the last two seasons. That's when Richmond got bumped down to Double-A because of our dilapidated stadium.

The Diamond was built on the cheap. When it replaced Parker Field, the old stadium was as past due date as a Christmas wreath in March. Even in 1985 dollars, eight million wasn't much, and you get what you pay for. A hurricane blew part of the roof off. The outfield developed a sinkhole. A damn chunk of concrete the size of a football fell onto the stands. It might have hit someone, if the team had been more popular at the time.

The thing is, if you go to the stadium, it doesn't look like such a bad place. The corn dogs are still tasty. The seats are wide enough, and there's a little holder in front of you where you can put your beer. Most of the sight lines are good. Even if you don't know diddly about baseball, it's a nice place to take the kids and let them scream like banshees, usually right in my ears, until the tykes tire out around the seventh-inning stretch and are carried out draped over their fathers' shoulders like bags of ketchup-stained cement.

The worst parts of The Diamond, where they figured nobody would notice a little corner cutting, are hidden away from the general public. Tops on that list would be the visitors' locker room. The home team's quarters are no prize, but nobody in the metropolitan Richmond area gives a damn how claustrophobic, mildewed and rat infested the visitors' digs are.

But, hell, the place still looks OK to me. When did it become accepted wisdom that baseball stadiums don't last as long as some Hondas?

Richmonders don't exactly have the high ground when it comes to goofy nicknames. Even in a league littered with SeaWolves, Baysox, two kinds of cats (Fisher and Rock) and, yes, the Curve, the Flying Squirrels stand out. Their bug-eyed mascot seems designed for the pre-K crowd, and it's hard to get a half inning in sometimes between all the PR stunts.

But the carnival acts do get people out to the ballpark. That's something. And the baseball's pretty good. A lot of these guys will bypass Triple-A, which has become kind of a retirement home for utility infielders, and go straight to the bigs.

It's opening night, and my companions are Jimmy Deacon and Cindy Peroni. Cindy certainly elevates the style and attractiveness of our party by quite a bit. Plus, she seems to know the history of most of the Squirrels. Between her and Jimmy, I have an overload of horsehide trivia pouring into each of my ears, sometimes simultaneously. I nod a lot.

It's been a busy day.

In the wee hours of the morning, when I should have been closing down Penny Lane, I got most of the rest of the sad story of the 1964 Richmond Vees. Using my pedestrian online research skills, usually employed only for Internet porn, I found Boney Bonesteel, Rabbit Larue and Buck McRae. Or, rather, I found out what happened to them.

Paul Bonesteel was thirty-three years old in 1964, playing out the string like Les. He hit .255 with ten home runs in the last year of a career that was only exceptional in that 99.9 percent of us guys who started out with big dreams in Little League never got anywhere near Triple-A to begin with.

He was smarter than most of the Vees, which made him, no doubt, a tall midget. But he had a college degree and, apparently, he had a pretty good career as a stockbroker, which started before he retired from baseball. And then, one spring evening in 1993, he was standing at a commuter rail station in the Long Island suburbs, perhaps after having a few pops at his favorite bar after a hard day ruining our economy on Wall Street. He was making a connection and evidently was alone at the platform when he lost his balance and fell in front of an incoming train. It was not, I'm thinking, an open-casket funeral.

In the news story I dredged up, Bonesteel's brother said Paul was a happy guy with a wife and two kids who loved him. He was going to retire that year. He also said he had the best balance of anyone he knew and could hold his liquor "like a champ."

There was no evidence of anyone seeing anything out of the ordinary before Bonesteel did his swan dive onto the tracks.

Rabbit Larue was the classic good-field, no-hit second baseman. Like Bonesteel, he never made it to the majors. Unlike Bonesteel, he didn't seem to have a great fallback position once he realized baseball wasn't going to love him back.

Information was scarce, but I did learn that he returned to the north Georgia town where he grew up. He was only forty-eight years old in 1990, when he disappeared. Whatever work he did after he retired from the game wasn't worth mentioning in the obituary. In the photograph, he looks worn out.

The obit said he was hiking a stretch of the Appalachian Trail near his home, something that was listed as one of his passions. He would go out for three or four days sometimes, his daughter said, and refused to let anyone know where he planned to go.

"He'd just say he was going walking," was her only quote.

I couldn't find any mention of his body being found. Actually, there wasn't any mention of anything about James "Rabbit" Larue anywhere in the ether after he disappeared. He was just gone.

I did find a live one. Buck McRae is still among us, or at least he was as of about a year ago. He lives in or near Fayetteville, North Carolina. He seems to be having a pleasant dotage, according to a feature the paper there did on him, with a loving wife and six kids, all still alive and living near him. There was a video accompanying the story.

As of a year ago, Buck still had his hand in the game, helping coach one of the American Legion teams. The hook for the interview was Jackie Robinson Day. The reporter asked him all kinds of stupid-ass questions about what it was like to be an African-American playing in 1953, when Buck signed a big-league contract and got sent to Brunswick, Georgia.

"We weren't African-American back then," McRae reminded the reporter. "We were colored, and that was on a good day. And there wasn't many good days."

What I read about and saw of Buck McRae, I liked. He appeared to have as many smile creases as frown wrinkles. I see on my map that I can get to Fayetteville to talk with him in a little more than three hours.

It's a pretty sorry list I've come up with. The 1964 Richmond Vees starting lineup has mostly retired from breathing.

Opening-day pitcher: Phil Holt died in a holdup in 1985, when he was forty-five.

Catcher: Les is still with us, for now.

First baseman: Jack Velasquez is the only one I haven't been able to track down. He'd be seventy-five if he's still alive.

Second baseman: Rabbit Larue disappeared hiking the AT at the age of forty-eight.

Third baseman: Roy Haas died of a heart attack four years ago. He was seventy.

Shortstop: Lucky Whitestone was killed in a hunting accident in 1988. He was forty-seven.

Left fielder: Paul Bonesteel. Crushed under a commuter train in 1993. He was sixty-two.

Center fielder: Jackson Rittenbacker. Assumed to have drowned in Lake Michigan in 2001 at the age of sixty-one.

Right fielder: Buck McRae. Alive and well, at last report.

People die. Eventually, it could even happen to me. But six of the nine Vees starters are dead, and five of those at least did not go gently into that good night. Two were shot, one apparently drowned, one disappeared on the AT and one fell under a train. And, of course, there's Les, who has not been exactly immune to violence of late.

I have asked Ed Chenowith, our remaining researcher at the paper, to please try and find Joaquin Velasquez, whose last known whereabouts was south Florida. He said he'd see what he could do.

I slept from three to eight, awakened by Kate, who informed me that I could interview Raymond Gatewood today at ten.

"You're going to behave," she says, not asking.

"Yes, ma'am. I won't be packing."

"Hah. Well, I'm taking you at your word. Gatewood doesn't know that you're Les's, uh, whatever."

"Almost stepson."

"Yeah. Well, he doesn't know, or I doubt he'd be interested in talking to you."

We agree that I will not try to pinch Raymond Gatewood's head off and shit down his neck.

I get Andi to agree to take Peggy and Awesome over to the hospital if I'll pick them up later.

At the city jail, they checked me for lethal weapons. Kate was waiting for me.

"When you see this guy," she said, "you'll see what I mean. He's not competent enough to find his ass with both hands."

We were taken back to a room where Kate and I sat on one side of a desk, with Gatewood, manacled, on the other.

I have to say, he's a somewhat scary-looking dude. He's about six two, with brownish hair that resembles a rat's nest.

He looks amazingly fit for someone who obviously hasn't been keeping up his health-club dues, but his skin has that dark, leathery appearance you get from living outdoors in the winter. When he looks at you, he doesn't seem to be really looking at you, but at something a few feet behind your head, like you're not there, or he doesn't differentiate between chairs and human beings.

Kate had filled me in a little on his numerous trips to Iraq and Afghanistan and his discharge after he tried to strangle a captain who apparently offended him in some way.

"I think," Kate said, "that he was basically over there to kill people."

I observed that that's kind of what soldiers do in wartime.

"No," she said. "I mean up close and personal, and maybe not armed combatants, just people somebody thought might be thinking bad thoughts about the United States."

Well, somebody's got to do it. But he's definitely a candidate for a little post-traumatic stress, and I know how diligent the VA has been in getting these guys help, so I was thinking, yeah, this definitely is a son of a bitch who'd shoot somebody from the ninth-floor window. For him, it'd be a fucking nostalgia trip.

But I promised Kate I'd hear the guy out, have the hanging after the trial.

"Why won't they believe me?" he asked my ex-wife.

I was thinking, why would they? You still were wearing the same dumb-ass jacket you had on when you shot Les.

"Tell him about the coat," Kate said.

He didn't seem to know at first what she was talking about. And then he did.

"Oh. Yeah. Like I'm lying there on my bench, tryin' to catch some rays, get out of the wind, you know? And I feel something hit my legs. I figure it's those damn college kids, fucking with me again. One of these days . . ."

"The coat," Kate said, interrupting.

"Oh. Well, I look down and there's this package balled up there at my feet. Some guy's walking away. I yell for him to come back, that he's dropped something, but he's moving pretty fast.

"Then I unwrap the package, and there's this coat. It was a little small for me, but, hey, beggars can't be choosers."

When he smiled, I could see that he was missing a couple of front teeth.

"So," I asked him, seeing Kate's look of annoyance at my breaking in, "what did you do with the wig? Why not wear that, too? It'd keep your head warm, maybe."

He looks at me like I'm speaking Swahili.

"Wig?"

"Wig. The one you wore when you shot Les Hacker."

Maybe I said it with a little more heat than I meant. Maybe that's why Kate kicked me.

"I don't know anything about a damn wig. I don't know what you're talking about, man. And I didn't shoot nobody. I did all my killing over there, protecting you pussies. And I didn't have to use a damn rifle every time, either."

Gatewood said he wore the coat a couple of days. Then, out of nowhere, "a bunch of mean cops threw me to the ground and kind of fucked me up."

He pointed to the missing teeth.

"They're goin' to have to get me a partial plate," he said. "And then I'm gonna sue their asses."

He put his cuffed hands on the table. He looked like he wanted to rip them off and mess somebody up. I wasn't sure he couldn't do it.

"Get this straight," he said. "I didn't shoot anybody. Man left me a coat, and I was glad to get it. If I knew all the shit that was going to come out of this, I'd of run the bastard down and made him take his coat back."

I asked Gatewood if he got a look at the man.

"Nah, just his back. He was just some guy."

We talked some more, me mostly trying to get him to slip up and admit that he knew about the wig, but my heart wasn't in it. If he was dumb enough to wear the same jacket he used for the shooting, in the damn shadow of the Prestwould, from Thursday to Monday, it seemed highly unlikely that he would be smart enough to pretend he didn't know anything about the wig.

When I asked him how he got hold of the key, he seemed equally adamant about his ignorance.

"C'mon," I said. "You know you took the key out of that vase and opened the door with it."

"I don't know anything about any fucking key, and I don't know anything about any fucking vase. You people are crazy."

We were winding up when he pointed to my finger.

"VCU grad?" he asked.

I told him that, yes, I was. An alumnus in good standing, good for twenty bucks a year to the mass comm school, come rain or shine.

"Me, too," he said.

Raymond Gatewood then proceeded to tell us what I can only assume he hadn't told the cops yet. He was class of '05, majoring in history.

"But, then, you know, I thought it wasn't right, not doing my part. I'd hear these big mouths, talking about how we ought to go over there and kick bin Laden's ass and blast 'em all back to the stone ages, and it kind of made me sick. I thought, if you're not going to do it, don't talk about it. So I did it."

I know what he means. We do have an overabundance of alligator mouths and hummingbird asses in the land of the free.

Gatewood rubbed his forehead. He looked tired.

Kate asked him if he was OK. He said he had a headache.

"Some days," he said, "I'm good. Some days, I'm not. Just the way it is. They say they're working on better drugs, but I tell you, all they do is make me sleep."

On the way out, Kate asked me if I thought it was possible that Raymond Gatewood somehow got hold of a Winchester .30-30, slipped into the Prestwould, found Finlay Rand's key, got into his unit and shot some guy in the park.

I told her that I thought just about anything was possible. I reminded her that Occam's razor usually shaves pretty smooth and clean.

"Do you think he's faking it?" she asked me. "Do you think he's playing crazy?"

I told her, no, actually it seemed more like he was trying to play sane.

"Well, you might be right there. He's lost it on a few occasions."

She ticked off some of the highlights: three assaults, one malicious wounding, one indecent exposure when he decided to celebrate spring two years ago by running around naked in the park.

"But here's the thing," she said. "Not one of those involved anything more complicated than the shoe he used to beat some bum who tried to rob him."

"Why isn't he in jail now?" Our jail is full of people who didn't do anything more violent than sell a narc a couple of ounces.

Kate laughed, but just with her mouth.

"They don't want him in jail. Hell, nobody wants him any-where. He tried living with his brother out in Chesterfield for a while, but he got out of control. The brother kicked him out, and you know what some deputy down there did?"

I think I know. I've heard this story before, just with dif-ferent characters. But I let Kate continue.

"They put him in a squad car and dropped him off in the park. Told him to keep his ass out of the county."

The suburbanites love to make jokes about Richmond's homeless population. I know, from doing a story or two over the years, that a lot of them are residing in our parks because those same suburbs gave them a one-way ticket here.

I was noncommittal, but I had to admit that my mind was a little more open than it was before I met Raymond Gatewood. I'm not quite so ready to start erecting the scaffolding just yet. Gatewood seemed either too crazy to do everything necessary to put his ass in that ninth-floor window with a high-powered rifle or too smart to go around wearing that plaid jacket in plain view of the crime. Damn facts. They keep getting in the way of my righteous anger.

Kate asked me how my opus on the '64 Vees was coming. I looked to see if she was being a smart-ass, calling it an opus. I couldn't tell. I filled her in on the team's diminishing numbers.

"Weird," she said. "Well, athletes tend to live closer to the edge than most of us."

Yeah, I said. Maybe that's it.

I promised her I'd check in with her after I got back from my trip.

"What trip?"

I told her about my just-hatched plan to fly to Tallahassee, Florida, and see if I could find some Whitestones.

Getting reacquainted with Cindy Peroni was better than a winning lottery ticket. It turns out that Cindy's brother flies for one of our more-maligned airlines. It further develops that Cindy "and a friend" can fly places for a very reasonable price—like, zero—if there's a seat. So, when I mentioned that I needed to fly some places and see some people, she made me an offer. If the gods are kind, we'll be flying down to Florida tomorrow, then driving over to south Alabama the next day.

"Can't I pay you something?" I asked her when she made the offer.

"I'll take it out in trade," she said. I said it might take me a long time to pay her back "that way" for a last-minute airline ticket. At my age, I'm more into comfort than speed.

"Well," she said, patting my arm, "just do the best you can."

Kate listened to my plans for tomorrow with what looked suspiciously like a smirk.

"Well," she said, "at least this one's age appropriate."

"I've never broken the law," I remind her.

"Not quite." Kate always has to have the last word.

I HAD time to look in on Les before the game. Peggy was still there. Awesome, never comfortable in one place for long, had disappeared someplace. I offered to take my mother home, but she said she was going to stay awhile longer.

"Want me to bring you anything?"

She looked up at me, giving me that wry smile she always was able to summon when we were being evicted or she'd lost another job.

"A joint would be nice."

We both laughed. I kissed the top of her head and left before guilt made me miss the season opener.

JUMPIN' JIMMY'S still on the payroll, like he has been for more than half a century, but he's mostly taking care of the field, getting it ready for the next home stand, recruiting kids to help roll the tarp out if it rains. In actuality, Jimmy mostly just sits on a riding lawn mower and tells everybody else what to do. I guess age has its privileges.

So, unless we have a rain delay, Jimmy's free to watch the game with us.

Cindy's deeper into baseball than I ever was, which is saying something. She and Jimmy get into a long, philosophical discussion over why pitchers are such "wusses," to use Cindy's description.

"I mean, those guys in the seventies were pitching, like 300 innings a year. I don't think I'd even heard of a middle reliever back then. How come these guys can't start but every fifth game? What would Bob Gibson say?"

"I love it when you talk baseball," I tell Cindy, then remind her that she was eight years old in 1975, and not many eight-year-old girls would have heard of middle relievers.

"Well," she says, "I was precocious. And I had older brothers."

Jimmy's definitely old, old school. But he tries to defend modern strategy, pointing out how they're throwing more exotic pitches now, and how much longer the games last.

"So," Cindy says, "they get tired standing out there on the mound? Hell, the games last so long because they've got to make so many pitching changes."

Jimmy sighs.

"They just go at it so much harder now, like every pitch is the World Series."

He's not buying into Cindy's other theory, that there are so many injuries now because the players are too muscle-bound.

"They got to stay in shape," Jimmy says. "Although I do think this yogi shit—pardon my French—is taking it a little too far."

"Yoga."

"Whatever."

There's a good crowd. They changed the grease in the corn dogs, just like they do before almost every season. And there'll be fireworks afterward.

The game itself is no prize. Through seven innings, nobody hits anything more impressive than a double into the right-center-field gap. There are too many walks and, yes, too many pitching changes. But it's still baseball. As I've gotten older, I've come to appreciate a game where you can catch your breath and analyze the situation between plays. Watching football, it's so intense your pants could be on fire and you wouldn't notice.

As we stand for the seventh-inning stretch, orchestrated by the demented tree rat mascot, Jimmy nudges me.

"I almost forgot. I gotcha something."

I put down my lukewarm beer and take the photograph Jimmy's handing me.

I know right away who it is. Frances Flynn.

"I found it, going through some old files," Jimmy says. Jimmy's files are legendary and notorious. He supposedly has two bedrooms of a three-bedroom apartment crammed with material about every Richmond minor leaguer since 1960. When he dies, they'll have to bring in a dump truck to haul it away.

"She was very pretty," I say, truthfully. She's squinting into the sun, with a big guy standing with his arm around her, low enough that he seems to be fondling her butt.

"That's Whitestone," Jimmy says, not pleasantly. "Must of been late in the 1964 season.

"I found this, too."

It's a letter.

"She wanted me to have it, so I could see how mean her mother was. I never gave it back. Hadn't looked at it in thirty years I bet, but talking about her the other day made me think of it."

The envelope was postmarked July 28, 1964. Jimmy says it wasn't long after Frannie Fling's parents found out where she was and what she was doing.

It's a pretty grim note. They gave her a deadline: September 1. If you aren't home by then, the note said, you do not have a home. There was enough chill in it to cool my beer.

"You have been a great disappointment to us," is how it concluded. It was signed by her mother.

The return address gave me her parents' names: William and Eleanor.

I already know she didn't go back until late fall or early winter, and I guess they relented, at least until they realized she was pregnant and kicked her out.

Andi's done some dumb things. I don't believe, though, that there's anything she could do that would make me toss her out the front door in the middle of a Vermont winter. I wonder how Mr. and Mrs. Flynn felt in April, when they were headed down to Tennessee to retrieve their daughter's body.

Cindy's been keeping score. They don't even want you to keep score at the ballpark any more, apparently. If they did, they wouldn't give you this tiny-ass scorecard and the kind of pencil you get at Putt-Putt.

There's something kind of endearing about the way she concentrates on the game and tries to make all the right marks in those too-small boxes. I take over for her when she goes to the bathroom.

The Squirrels pull it out when their fifth pitcher strikes out the Curve catcher with runners on first and third. The crowd has grown during the game, because of the fireworks. I note that this gives us a chance to get out quick, but Cindy says, "Oh, I love fireworks. Let's stay." So we do.

By the time I drop Jimmy off, it's after eleven. Our flight leaves at nine thirty in the morning.

"Maybe," Cindy says, "you ought to just come stay at my place. Might make it easier to get up and go in the morning."

I ask her if she has an extra bedroom. She looks at me like I'm an idiot and says she could make up the extra bed for me, if that's what I'd like.

I tell her that's definitely not what I'd like.

"Good," she says. "I don't have any extra clean sheets anyhow."

I stop by the Prestwould long enough to do some light packing while Cindy waits in the car.

Custalow looks up at me as I head out the door.

"Slut," he says. I give him the finger.

Chapter Nine

FRIDAY

*W*e're a little bedraggled this morning. My big brain, proponent of the benefits of a good night's sleep, didn't have much of a chance once we got in the front door of Cindy's place and she laid about a five-minute kiss on me. About two, though, I did have to beg for mercy, since the alarm was set for six thirty. "I'll Sleep When I'm Dead" is a great song, but the older I get, the less it seems like an intelligent life plan.

We are able to get on the flight to Atlanta, and we're able to get on the next one to Tallahassee. Apparently, when you have the kind of deal Cindy has through her brother, you spend a lot of time sitting in airport lounges holding your breath, hoping that you don't get bumped by a paying customer.

THE AIRPORT in Tallahassee is smaller even than Richmond's, and it doesn't take us long to rent a car and be on our way. Still, it's pushing one o'clock.

I have arranged an interview with Lucky Whitestone's son today at two, which gives us time to wolf down a couple of quarter-pounders. I promise Cindy that dinner will be an improvement.

"It'd almost have to be," she says, trying to restrain a ladylike burp.

The plan is to learn all I can about the late Mr. Whitestone today, then drive to south Alabama tomorrow, former home of the equally late Phil Holt.

Randall Whitestone Jr., age forty-two, lives on the north side of town. His home backs out onto a lake. He apologizes for the mess. Even by the low bar Custalow and I have set for bachelor living, the place is a wreck. Maybe Randy Whitestone isn't renting from his ex-wife, who, he informs us, took off last year. The Chinese take-out cartons on the dining-room table definitely need to be taken out.

He's not quite sure what I'm there about. I fill him in, trying to make it sound like a sensible mission rather than a fool's errand.

"Don't know why you'd want to do that," he says, shaking his head.

But he fills me in as best he can. Cindy, who has a knack for going from stranger to old friend in about two seconds flat, is in the kitchen, cleaning. Whitestone doesn't seem to mind.

He's kind of a classic example of the curse of the athlete's son. (OK, let's be PC and say athlete's child, but, I'm telling you, it really falls on the sons. Just the way it is.) He's built like his dad, or probably was before he started putting on a couple of pounds a year. He was, I found out on Google, a pretty good college baseball player at Florida State. He even had a year in Rookie League before giving up professional baseball for the exciting world of pharmaceutical sales.

But there was some little thing missing. Maybe he didn't quite have the reflexes his dad did. Or he was just a quarter step slower or didn't have a naturally perfect swing. Or maybe he had it a little bit easier growing up than Lucky Whitestone did. Maybe he didn't spend quite as much time outdoors in the summer, because who needs that crap when you have air conditioning?

At any rate, it really ought to be against the law for professional athletes to name their kids "Junior." I'm thinking Randall Whitestone Jr. has had to answer a whole shitload of questions in his life along the lines of, "How come you aren't a big-leaguer, like your daddy?"

"I was eighteen," he says. "It changed everything. I mean, he wasn't anybody's nominee for father of the year, but he was here. He didn't beat us. Well, maybe once or twice, but we deserved it. He taught me what he knew, even if I wasn't ever going to be as good as him."

Lucky Whitestone had gone out hunting that October day.

"The guys he hunted with, they were real careful. I don't think any of them ever would have mistook a man for a deer. They said they didn't, and I believe 'em. But the cops, they never found anything else. Might've been some asshole a quarter-mile away, maybe didn't even know what he'd done 'til he read it in the paper the next day. And those woods were full of shotgun shells."

Nobody ever came forward.

"It just kind of leaves a hole."

He says his father's old hunting buddies are still around, most of them.

"Some of 'em would come by, take me to football games and such, for a while, but it just, you know, got kind of awkward."

I ask him if he has kids. He says he has a girl, sixteen, and a boy, fourteen, both living with their mother most of the time.

"Is the boy going to be a baseball player?"

"Yeah," Whitestone says. "He's pretty good. Maybe it skips a generation."

I note that the fact that he played any pro baseball at all put him ahead of all the rest of us who topped out at Little League.

He grimaces.

"Well," he says, "it isn't quite up to what was expected around here."

Randall brings in a scrapbook, showing me the highlights of his father's baseball life, along with a few photos that were taken after he retired.

He shows me a ball autographed by all the Indians in 1975, Lucky's last year. There's a picture of young Randall posing with Frank Robinson, their player-manager that year.

"There's not really a whole lot I can tell you," he says. "He liked to hunt and fish and drink. He wasn't much for telling war stories."

I ask him if Lucky ever mentioned any of his old team-mates on the Richmond Vees.

"To tell you the truth," he says, "I didn't even know he played in Richmond. I only knew him as a big leaguer, and by the time I was in preschool, his days were just about over."

We talk for a while longer, and then I collect Cindy, who's just about salvaged the place.

"She can stay," Randall Whitestone says. "I like her."

"Me, too," I tell him.

My other tasks for the day are taking Ms. Cindy Peroni out for a meal we don't have to eat in the rental car and making a call to Folsom, California, to one Brenda Haas.

I let Cindy pick a restaurant. She says her brother, the bon vivant airline pilot who's always flying to exotic places like Tallahassee, recommends a place called A La Provence. He probably recommended it because he didn't have to pick up the tab.

OK. It was a good meal. I had the grouper; she had the duck breast. I made her grimace when I ordered the onion "soupe" and asked the waitress if it was French. And we did have the best crème brûlée I've had in my admittedly short experience with desserts that have little umbrellas over their names. And the wine, while it cost multiple times what I can get the same bottle for at Kroger's, was more than passable.

We get back to the Marriott Courtyard by nine, making it six Pacific time, when I've told Brenda Haas, via e-mail, that I'd call her. Roy Haas's widow, who probably is in her early seventies by now, answers on the third ring.

I explain what I'm doing, and she seems a little more on board with it than Randall Whitestone Jr. did.

She and Roy met during his brief stint in college and were "together" on and off for four years. They didn't get married until after he hurt his knee in spring training in 1965 and saw his big-league career die before it was even born.

"He seemed like he knew he had to grow up then," Brenda Haas says. "He really started applying himself."

Roy Haas went to work for a builder and eventually started borrowing money to buy up rentals all around Sacramento. By the time he died, his widow says, he had fourteen different properties.

"He was good at fixing things. He probably saved a million dollars over the years doing his own plumbing work and even some of the electrical stuff. He was still working like a dog, right up to the end, and he'd just turned seventy.

"But, you know," she says, "I think he was always a ballplayer, in his heart. We'd go to a game now and then, and he'd get this look like some kid standing outside a candy store, with his nose up against the window. After a while, we just didn't go anymore."

He'd had a minor heart attack a few years earlier, but he seemed to be in good health, she says, before his sudden demise.

"But you never know. I guess this was the big one."

The "big one" hit Roy Haas while he was inside one of his rental units, replacing carpet in the bathroom after the last tenant had apparently let the stopped-up toilet overflow instead of calling Haas to get it fixed.

"They found him there, on the floor. He'd been there they figured for a couple of hours at least. Wasn't any reason to use a defibrillator."

She says there was nothing suspicious about Roy Haas's death, no need for any autopsy.

"Roy didn't have an enemy in the world, other than maybe a few tenants he'd evicted when they wouldn't pay the rent, and most of them didn't have enough gumption to kill anybody."

The Haases didn't have children. Brenda Haas says, though, that Roy has left her "pretty well fixed." It has been four years now, and she's thinking about moving in with her sister down in Orange County, if she can sell all those rental properties.

"I just don't have the backbone Roy did," she says. "I hate throwing people out in the street, and sometimes you have to."

She seems happy to reminisce about his days in baseball. Unlike Lucky Whitestone's son, she does remember Richmond and 1964.

"I stayed with him for a week that summer," she says. "That humidity just about killed me. How do you people live with that stuff?"

I ask her if she remembers any of the other players or if Roy stayed in touch with any of them.

"Oh, no," she says. "I don't believe Roy ever kept in touch with anybody, after he left baseball."

"I know it was a long time ago," I say, taking a stab in the dark, "but do you remember a girl named Frannie Fling, from that summer in Richmond?"

She's quiet for a few seconds.

"Oh, my gosh," she says finally. "Yes. I haven't heard that name since, I guess, 1965. Roy said the players used to joke about her, that she was some kind of groupie. I think I met her one time, so it would have been 1964. She killed herself the next spring, I think. Roy was in Toledo then, trying to rehab his knee, not that it did any good, and he wrote and told me about what happened to her. Frannie Fling. Boy, that's going back a long way."

It's probably not the best time to ask if Roy Haas had his turn at bat with Frannie. Besides, I pretty much know the answer to that one.

I'm just about ready to get off the phone. Cindy has slipped into something more comfortable, which is nothing at all. Duty calls.

But Brenda Haas still wants to talk, and I've found that some of my best information over the years has come at the end of interviews, when we're "just talking." Guards get let down. You remember things you didn't remember before, probably because you're not trying so hard to remember.

"You know," she says, "I didn't get any sympathy cards from anybody that knew Roy when he was playing. But I did get the damnedest thing in the mail. I wouldn't have thought much about it, except for the ones I got before."

I motion for Cindy to stop doing what she's doing, so I can concentrate.

"The ones you got before?"

"Let me back up. Three days after Roy died, I got this post-card. There wasn't anything on it except a bunch of numbers, most of them crossed out. And I remembered Roy getting other ones just like it, now and then, over the years, but maybe with not so many numbers x'ed out. Neither one of us knew what to make of them."

"Do you remember the numbers?"

"Not after all this time. But let me look. I saved all the cards people sent, and I probably put that in with them. Can you call me back?"

I ask her if a couple of hours later will be OK, and she says that'll be fine.

"OK," I tell Cindy. "As you were."

Later, I call Peggy on her cell phone to find out how Les is doing. She doesn't sound too good. I ask her if she's been home today. She says she hasn't, but that Awesome Dude has brought her something to eat. Andi's been by, too, as has Jumpin' Jimmy Deacon and a couple of people from the Hill.

"They're trying to get him up to do some physical therapy," she says, "but he doesn't really want to."

She holds the phone to Les's ear so I can tell him to get some physical therapy, dammit, that I'm counting on him. It's a hell of thing to say, but I have counted on Les. Everybody needs a father figure, even if some of us wait half a lifetime to find one worth keeping.

Peggy says he nodded his head. I tell her to get some sleep. They have a cot there in the room for her, something they just brought in today. What I imagine my poor mother needs right now is some of that medical marijuana that's becoming legal everywhere except Virginia.

"I told them I needed to be with him," she says. "I don't trust them to look after him."

I argue in vain that they've got him pretty much triple-teamed night and day, but I know what she means. I don't want to think about the unthinkable, but it's hard not to. A nurse told me one time that, in her experience, people who are slipping away want to do it without anybody watching. It's the friends and family who want to be there at the end, as if that will make things less painful for us than they naturally should be.

Cindy is beside me. After I hang up, we just lie there, cuddling, for an hour or so, until it's time to call Brenda Haas again.

"I found it," she says.

The postcard was, as she thought, among the sympathy cards she got four years ago and put away.

"Don't know why I saved them," she says. "I guess I thought I might take them out and look at them. I hadn't opened that box again until today."

I ask her exactly what the postcard says.

"It doesn't say anything. It's just these numbers. One through nine, like a list down the page. Most of the numbers are crossed out. Just the two and the nine, they're the only ones not crossed out."

I ask her about the postmark.

"It's El Dorado Hills. Local. No return address."

"And you say you got others, over the years?"

"Roy did. He showed me a couple of them, but neither one of us could figure out what to make of them. Sometimes, it'd be several years, and then he'd come in with the mail one day and say, like, 'Well, we got another postcard from the numbers man.' "

I ask her if the others had most of the numbers crossed out, too.

"I'm not sure. It was a long time ago."

After my second conversation with Brenda Haas, Cindy lays claim to my attention again. One of these days, I tell her, we're going to have to spend a night together that doesn't have an alarm clock at the other end.

Something wakes me up. The clock radio tells me, in numbers several inches high, that it's 3:17. This normally would be good news. I can get up, take a piss and be back in bed and be asleep again in five minutes. The worst news the digital numbers can give you is that the alarm's going to go off in ten minutes, because that's ten minutes you're never going to get back from the sandman. But 3:17? That's usually gold.

Tonight, though, something's bothering me. I didn't know it was bothering me until I woke up. Maybe it was a dream, or my subconscious, but that postcard somebody sent to Roy Haas has obviously been hiding in the bushes, waiting to jump my ass. Now it has my full attention.

Cindy's sleeping like a rock, snoring lightly, with her back turned to me. How, I wonder, did I ever in my brainless youth think that forty-five-year-old women were too old to be attractive? I slip out of bed, manage to find my pants, shirt and cigarettes in the dark and slip out the door.

The lobby is empty when I walk through. The clerk, who looks like a college student, is snoozing at the front desk. Outside, it's so humid that the car windshields are soaked. I follow the concrete walkway, lighting a Camel as I go. I've been trying to not smoke around Cindy, because being a smoker these days is right up there with eating raw garlic or not bathing on the how-not-to-get-laid scale. But I always think better when

I smoke, and the electric jolt that woke me up requires some Class-A thinking.

By the time I've sucked in two cigarettes' worth of carcinogens and done a couple of laps around the parking lot, I feel pretty sure I'm on to something. Maybe I can even get back to sleep, as long as I don't wake up the lovely and seemingly tireless Cindy Peroni.

First thing on the list tomorrow, even before we crawl back in that rental car and head west for Alabama, is another call to Randall Whitestone Jr.

Chapter Ten

SATURDAY

*R*andall Whitestone Jr. has no memory of his father ever receiving any kind of postcard with numbers on it. He even seems a little put out that I would wake him at eight o'clock on a Saturday morning to ask him about it. Must be a late sleeper.

I ask him if his mother's still living, and if she might have gotten anything like the postcards Roy and Brenda Haas received.

"I think you're nuts," Randy Whitestone says. "What the hell has this got to do with some story about a damn minor-league baseball team?"

It might mean nothing, I concede, but it might mean a lot. I don't really want to go any deeper than that right now with Lucky Whitestone's son.

Finally, he tells me that his mother is still alive, although she's married again, and been widowed again.

"But for God's sake," he says, just before he hangs up, "don't call her at eight o'clock, and don't tell her I gave you her number. She's pissed off at me enough as it is."

I check the Richmond paper online in the lobby and see that Sarah Goodnight had a full evening pinch-hitting on the cops beat. Two dead, one wounded in a too-usual overnight shootout on the South Side. It happened after one, which means a call to Sarah any time before noon probably would not be appreciated. It also means another freebie for the Internet, another reason for our web masters to crow about how fast our online "product" is growing without further explaining that they aren't actually making any money giving our shit away.

A year or so ago, Enos Jackson got a call from some bonehead who wanted to know why we couldn't get all the good stuff in the paper, the way "those fellas on the Internet do." Jackson says he used to try to explain about early deadlines and space and time to the unwashed when they'd ask dumbass questions like that.

"Now," he said, when he related the conversation to me, "I just tell them those fellas on the Internet are just smarter than us."

I⊤ TAKES us a little more than four hours to drive from Tallahassee to Mobile, then another half hour to find the little town where Phil "Wimpy" Holt was born and died.

His widow is expecting us. It's already summer hot by the time we get there a little past two. She takes us out on the back porch, screened to protect us from the mosquitoes, and brings us some iced tea. This far south, they don't even bother to ask if you want it with sugar. I think we're at the epicenter of the Diabetes Belt. The house is on a little lake, and the log out in the middle turns out to be Sally. Every community should have a pet alligator. Lurleen Edwards says Sally isn't really much of a danger "although I wouldn't advise letting a small dog run loose around here." I trust her, but I do glance toward the lake every once in a while.

Lurleen looks to be about seventy. She is attractive and well kept; it's very easy to see why she was a beauty queen in her prime. And she's kept herself in shape. There's a photo on the wall of her finishing a 10K last year. She married again a few years after her husband was killed. Her second spouse, Walter, is out on the golf course that runs through their community. I ask if Walter can outrun an alligator. Cindy kicks me under the table, but Lurleen just laughs.

"Oh," she says, as she passes a glass of sugar water to me, "Walter says you don't really have to be that fast, just faster than your partner. Gators can't handle but one at a time."

She's a nice lady, and I don't want to do a bull rush on what I'm here to find out. We spend an hour or so chatting about Wimpy Holt's career, interrupted occasionally by Cindy asking her about a particularly attractive knickknack or an interesting photograph.

"They call him Phil around here," Lurleen says. "He never did like that nickname." Can't blame him.

Finally, though, I get around to that night in 1985, the one that ended Phil Holt's career as a life form.

"He didn't really make that much money in baseball," his widow says. "And he didn't really invest it all that well. I'll be honest with you: we were living in a condominium that was just a teensy bit bigger than this porch and falling behind on the payments.

"But Phil was the love of my life. When he got killed, it just about took me with him. I never really got over that."

She asks me not to use the part about her late first husband's place in her romantic pecking order, so as not to upset Walter, who obviously has done all money can do to heal a broken heart.

Normally, I'm a hard-ass on people who tell me something and then don't want to be quoted. This time, though, I'll make an exception.

Phil Holt was, as I'd been told by Jumpin' Jimmy, managing a Kwik Mart, far from the bright lights of the majors. He'd have been forty-five that year, a good ten years away from the last paycheck he got in the bigs. He didn't quite make it to the Promised Land of free agency, where a guy who won fifteen games for the Detroit Tigers could pick up a few million by just showing up alive at somebody's training camp the next March.

"Oh, he tried all kind of things to make a buck," Lurleen says. "Amway. A baseball card shop. We finally went flat busted when some fella convinced him to take most of what we had left and plow it into a sports bar. Wimpy's. Well, you can imagine Phil hated the name, but it was right out by the interstate, where they get lots of traffic, and people still remembered his name. In all the ads and the TV commercials, they'd say, 'Come have a beer with major-league all-star Phil Holt.'

"Trouble was, Phil had a lot of beers with a lot of people who wanted to shake his hand, and he didn't spend a lot of time checking the cash register. The fella showed up one day and said they were broke, and there wasn't any way Phil could prove they weren't, although we heard later the same fella opened another sports bar up in Huntsville a year or so later. Phil was kind of naïve. And he didn't have a lot of patience. Walter says he didn't pay attention to the bottom line, which was true."

Lurleen stops and swallows. She seems to be about as close to losing her composure as she'll ever get.

"But he was something," she says, then pauses and waves her well-tanned right arm as if she's pushing the past away. "Let's move on."

The night it happened was in late October. Phil was working the night shift by himself. The kid who was supposed to come in and close the place down, so Phil could go home at nine, called in sick.

"I still see that boy. Well, he's a grown man now, obviously, and he still kind of avoids me, like he knows it might have been him instead of Phil."

She shows me the stories from the Mobile paper. "Ex-major leaguer killed in robbery." "Police seek suspect in Holt murder." "Man questioned, then released in Holt case." And then, a year later, "No new leads in Holt killing."

"They questioned this one fella, because he was seen in the same block and he had held up a liquor store and done time ten years before, but nothing ever came of it.

"And then, I think they just stopped looking."

The crazy thing, she said, was that almost nothing was taken from the register.

"He was good about locking the cash up in the safe every couple of hours or so," she says, "and there wasn't any sign that whoever shot him even tried to get at that. Phil wouldn't have gotten himself killed trying to protect the Kwik Mart's money, I can tell you that. And there wasn't any sign of a struggle."

Eventually, she said the police told her that it might have been some crack addict from Mobile or New Orleans just stopping to get enough money for a rock, and then he just got spooked or something and started shooting.

It's past four thirty when I get around to asking her about postcards.

I describe the kind of cards Brenda Haas says she's gotten over the years.

Lurleen gets a strange look.

"Yes," she says. With her sweet-tea accent, it comes out "Yay-uss." "There was a card, like what you're talking about. It came right after Phil's death, along with all the sympathy cards, just like she's talking about. I remember how peculiar it was, with no return address, just postmarked Mobile. And it did have those little numbers on it. It's just like she said, one through nine. And I think the one was crossed off. I got another one, just like it, maybe two or three years later, and I think that one had two numbers crossed off. Like maybe the one and the five or the six?

"I think that's all I got. It wasn't long after that that Walter and I started seeing each other, and then I moved."

She asks me why I'd ask about something like that. I tell her that I'm not sure, but that I will tell her what I know when I know something.

"If it's about finding who killed Phil," she says, lowering her voice as if the neighbors might be listening, "I'll do anything I can to help catch the son of a bitch."

Before we head out for what we've been told is the best fish camp in the general area, I make my call to Lucky Whitestone's widow back in Tallahassee.

She's been expecting my call.

Thelma Boyle is, I'm estimating, about the same age as Lurleen Edwards. She sounds a little more world-worn, though. She has a voice that sounds like it's been filtered through a few million cigarettes and a truckload of bourbon.

But she has what I need.

"Hell, yeah, I got them cards," she says. "Still gettin' 'em."

I ask for some more detail. The then-Thelma Whitestone says she got a postcard like the one Phil Holt's and Roy Haas's widows got right after Lucky's fatal hunting accident.

"But it wadn't the first one," she says. "I'd got one a couple of years before that. The one after Lucky got killed, it had two numbers crossed off. I don't remember about the first one.

"But the other ones, after that, they would have more and more numbers marked off."

I ask her how many she's gotten, over the years, and she says maybe six or seven. The last one, she says, was maybe four years ago.

"I remember that one, because it made me curious," she says. "It had everything marked off except the two and the nine."

She's heard from her son that I'm doing a story on some minor-league team Lucky played on. She says she can't really tell me that much, because she wasn't with him in Richmond.

"We'd dated and all," she says, "and we had sort of an understanding, but I never went up there. I'm sorry I can't tell you much more. Randy can tell you what you need to know."

I tell her that she's been a big help.

"Are you going to talk to Randy again?" Thelma Boyle asks me.

I say that I'm not sure.

"Well, if you do," she says, "tell him to get his butt over here and mow my damn grass. He promised to do it on Tuesday."

I HAVEN'T had anything of note to drink in the last two days. I've been so good that I decide to reward myself. Many of my problems over the years have started with me rewarding myself.

I have a couple of Early Times on the rocks while we wait for a table. Cindy nurses a glass of white wine that, tragically, comes from Alabama. Ever the trouper, she says it's not bad.

Another ET at the table and most of the bottle of chardonnay we're supposed to share, and I'm feeling good, although from the looks Cindy's giving me, maybe I'm not sounding and looking as good as I feel. She doesn't try to stop me from having another ET after our fish dinner. She doesn't even try to stop me from driving when we get in the rental car.

We're not half a mile down the road when the blue lights go off like some kind of state police light show in the rearview mirror. Heartsick, I pull over. I'm thinking this is the worst possible scenario. Being the son of a light-skinned African American, I seldom even think about race these days. I know we're not past it, but I've been a noncombatant in that sad, ridiculous war for a long time. I'm in the deepest South right now, though, and I'm feeling a major dose of paranoia coming on. Even if the state trooper thinks I'm some kind of Middle Eastern mélange, that has its own downside. Either way, it's DWIANW—driving while intoxicated and not white.

"Quick," Cindy says, already undoing her seatbelt. "Switch."

It is not one of the noble moments of my life, but I'm barely back to full driving status again after an unfortunate incident in downtown Richmond in which everyone but me seemed to be going the wrong way on a one-way street.

Somehow, we manage to switch seats and even buckle up before the state trooper ambles up and shines his light in Cindy's eyes.

"Have you been drinking, ma'am?" he asks her, as polite as a cat contemplating a canary. He looks over at me suspiciously. I look straight ahead.

"Two glasses of wine, officer," she says, and she's not lying by more than one. "I'm the designated driver. This one"—she points dismissively in my direction and shakes her head—"sure as hell wasn't going to be able to get me back to the hotel safely."

She's really laying the southern accent on thick. She dipped at least two states toward the equator.

He takes her driver's license, making a note that it's from Virginia, which probably qualifies as Up North down here. Then he hands it back.

Because she's minding her manners and is pretty, he doesn't make her get out and walk the centerline or recite the alphabet backward. He does, however, make her blow into the breathalyzer. I'm holding my breath, but Cindy doesn't seem fazed.

"How'd I do?" she asks the officer, bright as a penny.

He grunts.

"Good enough," he says, "but not by that much. You know, I could take you in anyhow."

"Oh," Cindy says, "I hope you don't. I need to get this jerk back to the hotel."

The trooper finally manages a smile.

"Well, you do that," he says. "And be careful out here. Don't want to have somebody as pretty as you get in an accident. You all be safe now."

He gives me one more look, like he's trying to figure out what the hell I am.

She thanks him, then slowly pulls out into the road. In the five minutes between there and the hotel, I don't say anything. All that blue-light adrenaline has gone a long way toward sobering me up.

Finally, in the parking lot, I clear my throat.

"Thank you."

I can't think of anything else to say. I feel like Mr. Johnson has shrunk about two inches. I am not feeling very manly.

"Don't worry about it," Cindy says, then turns off the ignition and turns to me.

"Willie," she says. "I'm not going to be a nag. I'm not going to be that person. We are who we are. I've got my faults, which I'm sure you'll discover if you stay around long enough. Andy warned me—well, not warned, maybe, but told me—that you can hit it pretty hard when you get going."

She's quiet for a few seconds. I'm waiting for the other shoe to drop like a block of concrete on my muddled head.

"Here's the thing, though. I'll never hound you, never ask you why you drink so much. But I'm forty-five, and I've been through some shit. If things get bad, if I come to think you're giving me insomnia and frown lines, I will leave, and I won't look back. Life's too short. That's not an ultimatum or a threat or anything like that. It's just the way it is."

She says it quietly, calmly.

"I'm sorry," I tell her. Seldom have I been more sincere in that sentiment.

"Don't be sorry," she says. "Be better. And get your ass out of the car. The night's still young."

Inside, though, the night gets a bit older.

I check my cell phone, which I can never hear in restaurants or pretty much anywhere else these days.

There's a call from Kate.

"Willie," the voice mail says, "call me. Now."

I do, and the news isn't good. At least, it isn't good for Raymond Gatewood.

For some reason, the cops didn't get around to giving Gatewood's jacket a good going-over until today.

"They found the key," Kate says, and I hardly have to ask which one.

The missing key from Finlay Rand's apartment, the one somebody took from the vase outside his door, turned up in Gatewood's coat pocket.

I observe that this might just about seal the deal. Let's get on with the hanging. I'm eager to put somebody on the scaffold, especially now, with Les holding on by a gnat's eyelash.

"Well," Kate says, "if he's telling the truth about somebody dropping the jacket and him picking it up, the key thing doesn't necessarily prove he was the shooter."

I tell Kate it's good enough for me until a better suspect comes along. And I'm pretty sure it's good enough for Richmond's finest and probably for the jury.

"It's late," I tell her. "I've got to go." And I hang up.

I fill Cindy in on what's happened.

"Sounds like they've got the right guy," she says.

"Maybe."

"Why only maybe? I mean, he was wearing the same clothes as the guy the camera caught leaving the building after the shooting, right? And he had the key in his coat pocket."

It's time to tell Cindy about the numbers.

"Holy shit," she says, when I've finished. "I should've figured that out, as many scorecards as I've filled out over the years."

"Well, sometimes things are so obvious you can't see 'em."

When Roy Haas's widow first mentioned the postcards, I made notes, mental and otherwise, but it didn't seem to be going anywhere. But then, when I called back and she told me there were nine of them, and which ones had been crossed out, I started to see the light.

I've never known why baseball scorecards list the players the way they do. I should look it up sometime. I mean, I can understand why the pitcher is No. 1 and the catcher is 2, and then it makes sense to make the first baseman 3 and the second baseman 4. But why skip over the shortstop and make the third baseman No. 5, then go back to shortstop for 6? And why go from right to left across the infield, then left to right, 7 through 9, in the outfield?

The only numbers not crossed out on Brenda Haas's last postcard were the 2 and the 9. Catcher and right fielder.

As far as I can tell, Buck McRae is still alive and kicking in North Carolina. And Les is still with us, for the moment.

I know Roy Haas, third baseman, had his heart attack four years ago. I know that Lucky Whitestone, shortstop, has been dead twenty-four years. I know that Phil Holt died in that convenience store holdup in 1985. I know Jackson Rittenbacker, center field, drowned in Lake Michigan eleven years ago, and that Rabbit Larue, second base, disappeared while walking the Appalachian Trail in 1990. I know about Paul Bonesteel, left field, who met his demise under a subway train in 1993.

All that leaves, in addition to Les and Buck McRae, is Jack Velasquez, the first baseman, and I'm not feeling too good about old Jack.

Most of the starters for the 1964 Richmond Vees seem to have met their fates, in a variety of ways and over a period of at least twenty-three years. It's not unusual for people to die. Happens all the time. And it's not unusual for former athletes to buy it while they were out hunting or fishing or walking the AT. But the only starters to get to their seventieth birthdays are Les, McRae and Velasquez, assuming he's still living.

All this combined misfortune might make a nice hook for my story. The Curse of Parker Field or some such shit.

There's only one thing that makes it more than a coincidence:

Somebody's keeping score.

Chapter Eleven

Sunday

*W*e barely make our flight out of Mobile at seven. I don't think I slept two hours, because Cindy was so jazzed up after I told her about the scorecards that she kept asking me questions.

I run into a men's room at the airport just before they start boarding us, and the glimpse I get of myself as I rush out, drying my hands on my pants, makes me wonder why Cindy Peroni, who could pass for thirty-five instead of forty-five even after forgoing sleep, is willing to spend a minute with me, let alone a weekend.

"Come on," she says, holding a place for me in line. "If we miss this one, we might have to drive back to Richmond."

We're lucky somebody or somebodies slept later than we did, late enough to miss their flight to Atlanta and forfeit their seats to us.

It's still shy of ten thirty when we get back home. We both agree that brunch at Millie's might be just the restorative we need.

They don't take reservations. Most of my favorite joints don't. There's a crowd milling around outside the place, young and old, black and white, hipster and Commonwealth Club, all undeterred by the roar of motorcycles as the two-wheel crowd descends on Poe's Pub down the street. The owner greets me and takes our names. One thing about Millie's: they never lose your name. You might wait an hour, but the guys who came in right after you will wait an hour and five minutes.

I'm into my second Bloody Mary and Cindy's switched from chardonnay to iced tea by the time they call us. On a nice spring day like this, it's almost a disappointment when you don't have to wait outside savoring the hair of the dog.

"Don't worry," I tell Cindy. "I'll take it easy."

"Your call," she says, shrugging.

Richmond's a big enough city to keep me entertained, but it's small enough that you never know when two of your little universes are going to collide.

And so it is that I look up just in time to see Awesome Dude headed toward us. Even among the eclectic mix waiting for a table, Awesome attracts attention. And, of course, he spies me immediately. I'm not saying I wouldn't have acknowledged him anyhow, but I don't have the chance.

"Willie!"

Everyone looks at me. I greet him the way you should greet the guy who's been at your mother's side in her hour of need. I give him a man-hug, noting to myself that he seems to have showered in the last three days. Cindy, who knows him from the hospital, asks him if he wants a drink.

He declines. He's on one of his walkabouts. Despite the fact that he has housing when he needs it in Peggy's English basement, Awesome is still a little on the feral side.

"How's Les?"

Awesome shakes his head.

"Aw, Willie," he says, "I don't know. He just stares up at the ceiling. He ain't got the will no more."

I tell him that my next stop is the hospital. He says he's just taking a break to clear his head. I avoid saying that it might take a way-back machine to do that. I can't remember when Awesome Dude's head didn't need clearing.

Just then, the owner sticks his head out the door and shouts, "Black!"

We start walking toward the door before we lose our slot and have to drink for another forty-five minutes outside.

"Wait," Awesome says, tugging at my sleeve. The way Awesome says it, sans a few teeth, it comes out as "Ait."

I tell Cindy to go on and secure our table.

I wait.

"That fella, the one they said shot Les?" Awesome says.

"Yeah?"

"I know him. He ain't like that."

I'm aware that Raymond Gatewood's nonmilitary record seems to stop short of actual killing, but maybe Awesome, who spends more time on Richmond's streets than a stray dog, can tell me something I don't know. It's my experience that everybody can teach you something, if you just shut the hell up and listen.

It turns out that Mr. Gatewood has spent some time in the same homeless hangouts as Mr. Dude. Awesome, who is a better observer of human nature than most of his species when he's not drug-addled, has seen the bad side of Les's accused shooter.

"He'll fuck you up," Awesome says, speaking a little louder than your average brunch goer and getting a quick glance or two from the assembled. "But if you don't mess with him, he don't mess with you. I never seen him start nothing. And Les, he dudn't mess with nobody."

No, he dudn't. I thank Awesome for his insight and bid him bon voyage, stopping short of asking him inside to share our table. I care for Awesome, but I don't want to do anything to mess up my status at Millie's.

I find Cindy, sipping a black coffee and studying the board.

I pass on Awesome's information. I also thank Cindy for not high-hatting a guy the whole world has high-hatted.

"You don't know when that might be you," she says.

One Cajun mess and a crab enchilada later, we leave for the hospital.

Peggy, Andi and Jumpin' Jimmy are there when we arrive, along with a couple of characters who used to do roofing for Les. I think Peggy's glad to have a crowd here. She looks like she's lost a pound a day in the ten days Les has been here, and my dear old mom didn't have any weight to lose. Peggy's always been running at a higher gear than most of us, enough to burn off the effects of half a century of the munchies.

We step outside for a couple of minutes to let some of the others carry on one-sided conversations with Les. Jumpin' Jimmy seems capable of holding up his end of the conversation for hours.

"I don't know if he's going to make it," Peggy says. "You know, I even prayed, for whatever good that'll do."

It can't hurt, I tell her.

"I told whoever's up there that I promise I'll take care of Les, no matter what shape he's in. I just want him back."

I give her a hug. She's snuffling against my shirt. I assure her that Les is going to get better. The hope of the hopeless is better than no hope at all.

I manage to have a few words with Jimmy. As quickly and simply as I can, I tell him about what I found out in Florida and Alabama. When I tell him about the scorecards, he's about as speechless as Jumpin' Jimmy Deacon ever gets.

When I start to go back inside, Jimmy grabs my sleeve.

"So, you think maybe that asshole, excuse my French, they got locked up has been killing ballplayers?"

I tell Jimmy that I doubt it, that whoever did it, if one person did, has been doing a lot of traveling, and he's been at it for, by my count, twenty-seven years. Twenty-seven years ago, Raymond Gatewood would have been about six years old.

I warn Jimmy that this all could just be a string of coincidences, but when he asks me if it was a coincidence that everybody was getting those scorecards, I didn't have an answer for him.

"But why?" Jimmy says. And I don't have an answer for that one, either.

We stay a couple of hours. I drop Cindy off at her house, thanking her again for all she's done for me, including saving me from my second DUI in less than two years.

"You got lucky when you found me," she says. "Maybe I got lucky, too. Don't screw it up, Willie."

BACK AT the Prestwould, I have a message to call Finlay Rand. That can wait, though.

There are two more calls on my list. I've already tried Rabbit Larue's daughter once, and no one answered. And I want to talk to Paul Bonesteel's brother, the closest relative I could find.

Still no answer at the daughter's house, but Anthony Bonesteel himself, residing in Babylon, Long Island, answers on the third ring.

It takes me awhile to get across to him what I'm trying to do. From the information I got online, Paul Bonesteel's older brother is eighty-four or eighty-five years old, and his hearing's not so great.

Being a lifelong Yankees' fan, he finds the story of how the Richmond farm team had to be called the Vees amusing.

"You guys," he says, and I can hear a kind of creaky, old man's laugh. "You never got over losing the war, did you?"

I concede that this might be the case, at least with some of my fellow citizens.

Once I get him started, though, he's willing, even eager, to talk about his brother.

"Paulie, he was like a god. He always made straight As in school, was always the best at whatever sport he played. I told him he should oughta stick to football, but he said he'd last longer in baseball. Hah!"

Paul Bonesteel, "Boney" to his teammates but not to any of his family back home, was just about done in 1964, his fourth year in Triple A with nothing but a cup of September call-up coffee with the big team to show for it.

"But he was smart. He got his degree while he was playin' ball, and then he went to work on Wall Street, and he made a killing."

Paul Bonesteel's wife, I learn, moved back to her hometown, Atlanta. Their kids, already grown when Paul died, live in the Atlanta area, too. He gives me her address and phone number.

"Tell her to call me once in a while."

I ask Anthony about the way his brother died.

He's quiet for a few seconds. I hear him clearing his throat.

"He didn't fall on no damn train tracks," he says. "He had the best balance of anybody I ever seen. And they said he was maybe drunk. Paulie never got drunk. He could drink like a champ, and he might should of slowed down. He'd put on some weight. But nobody never, ever saw Paulie Bonesteel drunk."

I wait for it.

"He was pushed. That's all there was to it. The cops didn't want to hear that. Too damn much trouble, I guess. But he didn't fall, and I can tell you, sure as shit, he didn't jump. Paulie and Barbara were together almost thirty years, raised two kids. They were like lovebirds."

I ask him who would do such a thing.

"I don't know. Nobody knows. Some maniac. Some kid fucked up on drugs. I hope he's rotting in hell, whoever he is."

Anthony Bonesteel talks awhile more about his brother, filling me in on his childhood and the knee injury that kept him from being a big leaguer.

"The year they brought him up in September, it was 1962. They'd already clinched the pennant and was going to play the Giants in the World Series. We all went to the stadium, must have been twenty of us, aunts and uncles, Mom and Pop were still alive then, cousins. And Paulie got to pinch hit in the seventh inning, and he got a single, a frozen rope to right field. But he was already too old, and he was damaged goods, with that knee."

I ask Anthony if he'd ever heard his sister-in-law, or Paul himself, say anything about getting some kind of postcard with numbers on it. He says he's never heard of such a thing, and asks me why the hell I asked such a stupid-ass question. I don't see much point in telling him about the scorekeeper, at least not right now.

I TRY the number in Dawson, Georgia, again. This time, a somewhat frazzled-sounding woman answers.

"Crystal Scoggins?"

"Yeah. Who is this?"

I try to explain. Although Rabbit Larue's daughter seems to have no hearing issues, I have trouble getting my idea across to her.

"Is this going to cost me anything?" she asks, "'cause if it is, you can hang the hell up right now. Jackson Lee! Get off that coffee table!"

I assure her that I'm not trying to get money from her, and also assure her that she won't be getting any from me. She seems to accept this break-even proposition.

She explains that she's looking after her grandchildren and has to stop occasionally to yell at them and threaten them with various forms of corporal punishment.

Finally, I get her talking about Rabbit.

"Daddy was something," she says. "Momma said he didn't ever want to do nothin' but play baseball. He tried his hand at this and that after he quit playing, but his heart just wasn't in it. I was just a baby when he quit, and after that I just remember him sitting around the house a lot, and just disappearing for days at a time, whenever the mood struck him."

He was forty-eight when he took his last trip. Crystal, who was then married to her first husband, was living in a trailer on the edge of Larue's property. She said neither she nor her mother thought that much about it until Rabbit had been gone for three days.

"He was always back in three days or less," she says. "When it got up to five, we called the sheriff."

Rabbit Larue just disappeared. No note, no trace, nothing.

"There was all kinds of rumors," Crystal says. "Some of the meaner folks said he'd had a girlfriend off somewhere and had left to be with her. Like Momma didn't feel bad enough as it was. But we never believed that. For sure, he wasn't no angel, but he never hit us unless we deserved it, and he did the best he could.

"And he wouldn't of been the first fella to disappear on the AT, won't be the last."

It takes me about forty-five minutes to get to what has become the big question.

"You mean, like a regular postcard?" Crystal says. "With little numbers on the back?"

I tell her that's what I'm talking about.

"Yeah. . . . Yeah. That's funny. Momma did get one like that. She might not of remembered it, except she got one just like it, maybe three years later, and then two or three times more over the years, before she died, back in 2007."

I ask her if any of the numbers were marked through.

"Yeah," she says. "She'd show 'em to me, and it seems like, thinking back, that there was more numbers crossed through every time."

Any of those postcards, Crystal assures me, would have been thrown away long ago.

"We just went up in the attic and pitched everything. It was just junk, anyhow, and we ain't got anywhere to store any of it in the apartment."

Crystal Scoggins is again distracted by her grandchildren, who seem to be doing something untoward with the cat. I thank her and hang up.

CUSTALOW'S IN the living room when I come in from my afternoon telethon.

I tell him what I know.

"And you think all those guys dying and disappearing is connected to Les being shot?"

"What would you think?"

"Well," he says, "it does seem like somebody had it in for the Vees. But it doesn't make much sense, does it?"

No, it doesn't.

I have a couple of High Lifes with Custalow and then make my final call of the day, this one in person.

I have to buzz twice before Finlay Rand answers his door. He thanks me for coming. His manners are as immaculate as his dress pants, starched shirt and silk sports jacket. I imagine Rand wakes up crisp.

He offers me some white wine, troubling himself to tell me exactly what part of the Loire Valley it comes from. He's using crystal. From sad experience during my conjugal days with Kate, I've learned that people don't like it when you break their crystal, so I move with great caution. I have to admit, though, the wine does not suck.

After a brief but tedious amount of chitchat, Rand gets to the point.

"I think somebody is after me," he says, taking a small sip and setting his glass down.

"After you?"

"You know, I told you—asked you—not to put my name in the paper. And now, I've started getting these calls."

I wait.

"Whoever it is says he's a friend of that man, the one who broke into my apartment. He said that if I don't drop the charges against the man, he'll make sure something bad happens to me."

That's ridiculous, of course. Whatever grievances Finlay Rand might have against Raymond Gatewood pale in comparison to attempted murder, which will move on up to murder if Les doesn't pull through. And any friend of Gatewood's would know whose apartment he broke into, with or without verification in the newspaper. A visit to or phone call from Gatewood would do the trick.

I explain this to Rand, who is far from mollified.

I ask him if he's called the cops about this.

"No," he says after a brief hesitation. "The man on the phone said I'd better not do that, either."

I tell Rand that I know Gatewood's defense attorney, and that I can ask her to have a chat with the accused, perhaps emphasizing that any future threats that can be traced back to him will only make his sorry plight worse. I can also check and see who has visited him at the city lockup.

"Well," he says, "if you think that would help."

Despite the fact that you could keep meat in here, Rand is sweating a little. I see the little half-moons on the armpits of that fresh shirt and wonder how many of those he goes through a day.

He clears his throat.

"Do they think, uh, do they think they'll be able to wrap everything up soon?" he asks.

I tell him I'm not sure. I mention some of the more troublesome aspects of the case against Mr. Gatewood, such as his seeming lack of either the want-to or the wits to do what was done to Les. I don't mention the fate of the 1964 Richmond Vees starting lineup.

Maybe, I say, he was telling the truth when he claimed somebody left that jacket on a park bench.

"Perhaps so," Rand says. "But he certainly seems to have some malevolent friends."

Rand shows me a couple of paintings he's just bought from an estate sale.

"They were an absolute steal," he says, and I'll have to take his word for it. He says they're abstract. They must be, because I wouldn't know whether they were upside down or sideways. Kate always said my idea of high art was Dogs Playing Poker, but I can appreciate a velvet Elvis.

I promise to have a quiet chat with the defense attorney. Rand surprises me when he says he imagines the fact that she's my ex-wife might carry some weight.

"It's a small town, Mr. Black," he says to my unasked question. I think I see the hint of a smirk, but maybe it's just a nervous tic. Well, if Finlay Rand is smart enough to afford the Prestwould and silk jackets, he can't be as dumb as he seems.

Chapter Twelve

MONDAY

*N*ormally, even if I weren't on the world's shortest sabbatical, I wouldn't be here today. My days off, since I got busted back to night cops, are Sunday and Monday. My Saturday nights often don't start until Sunday morning. But I try to make up for lost time.

Today, though, Ed Chenowith says he has some news for me. Ed once worked in the morgue, when we had one. Now, he's a researcher in the newsroom. They let the whole library staff go, then hired Ed back, at two-thirds what he was making before, to, as he so eloquently puts it, "find shit." He felt guilty about taking a job from the people who gutted his department, knowing the rest of his former associates were drawing unemployment or working at Walmart, but mortgage payments trump conscience every time. Ed's good at what he does, though. He knows how to go deep, miles below the Google searches and Wikipedia biographies that pass for research among the reporting class these days.

It's funny. We used to have to work the phones harder than a telemarketer on commission. That's how you "found shit." Now, most of it's at our fingertips. The only problem, and I've seen it happen even with the talented Sarah Goodnight, is that younger reporters aren't really communicating, getting to know their sources. Their sources are websites. I wonder often, sometimes out loud, if people younger than forty are losing the ability to communicate via eye contact and vocal chords.

And, of course, they wonder when antiques like me are going to stop boring them to death with stories about how it used to be before the earth's crust cooled.

"How old are you, anyhow?" one smart-ass metrosexual asked me one day last month when I was fascinating myself by giving a brief, unsolicited history of pneumatic tubes.

Still young enough, I reminded him, to kick his ass. Unfortunately, he took my jovial riposte seriously, and I had some 'splainin' to do to the HR folks, whose job it is to correct our antediluvian tendencies.

I'm surprised to see Sarah also in on a Monday. Since she's covering for me until I finish with the Vees project, she should be doing something worthwhile today rather than working.

"Oh," she says, sighing, "I still have to get that damn feature done, the one on the ninety-year-old identical twins."

"Yeah, there might be a time element on that one."

"They could go any minute," she says. "I mean, ninety probably seems old even to you."

When I give her a dirty look, I see the hint of a smile.

"It's really cruel to torture old people," I tell her.

"I know. But I just can't help myself. It's just too easy."

Ed Chenowith is sitting in the little broom-closet office they've made for him. The library used to be on a separate floor. When they brought Ed back, it seemed easier to put him in the newsroom. But he wanted to be able to shut the door from time to time, because reporters were asking him to do everything but wipe their butts. The last straw was when Wheelie found out the sports guys were leaning on him to set up a program for their fantasy baseball league. So Wheelie took one of the old one-on-one interview rooms and stuck him in there. He can lock the door from the inside.

Ed's not very chatty, but he and I get along well. I used to spool my own microfilm reels, which qualified me, compared to most of my compatriots, for the Nobel Prize for Not Being Aggressively Needy.

"That guy," he says, "the one down in Florida? I think I found what you need."

Joaquin "Jack" Velasquez, the 1964 Vees' slick-fielding, banjo-hitting first baseman, was from Mexico. He returned there not too many years after his season in Richmond, where a .288 batting average and a nimble glove were not enough to offset a mere five home runs.

"He was somethin' diggin' balls out of the dirt," Jumpin' Jimmy Deacon said in his assessment of Velasquez. "But you know, good fielding first basemen, they're like tall midgets."

What Ed Chenowith has found is what is almost certainly the last chapter of our former first sacker's checkered life.

Velasquez, according to the records Ed's been able to locate, moved back to the States sometime in the early nineties.

He was arrested twice in the Fort Myers area, once for possession and once for possession with intent to distribute.

"He got sent back after he did twelve months in prison.

"But then, he must have come back again."

This time, in 1996, Jack Velasquez wasn't arrested. He was sliced and diced.

"They made the ID based on a tattoo," Ed says, showing me the documentation. "Part of him, his torso apparently, washed up somewhere on the Gulf coast, and they found a tattoo of his Social Security number on his chest, from back when he was playing ball here, I guess. They never found the rest, but they were pretty sure it was Velasquez."

Yeah, odds are you wouldn't tattoo somebody else's SSN on your body. Putting your own number there also seems counterintuitive, though. I mean, you couldn't remember it?

"So, did anybody ever get arrested for impersonating a butcher?"

Ed shrugs.

"Apparently not. There didn't seem to be a lot of follow-up, from what I can find."

I tell Ed he's found plenty and promise to buy him a drink sometime.

"I could use it," he says, then goes on to vent a little about Mark Baer.

"The son of a bitch," he says, lowering his voice, "wants me to go county by county, locality by locality, through the whole state and get numbers on all the people who were arrested for going more than ninety miles an hour last year. I think he's trying to win the Pulitzer for highway safety coverage."

I can relate. Baer used to ask me, every time he went anywhere on company business, how to fill out an expense form. Again, aggressive neediness.

So, I'm thinking maybe Velasquez decided to become a drug entrepreneur, and maybe he ran into some guys who had their MBAs in evil. Poor Jack Velasquez. Good field, no hit, no brain.

And then there were two. Les and Buck McRae, whom I'm going down to North Carolina to see tomorrow.

Time to talk to the chief.

I call Peachy Love, police flack and former reporter, and ask her what my chances are of talking with our police chief, Larry Doby Jones, sometime today.

"I don't know," she says, but I tell her that I have some evidence that Raymond Gatewood might not be Les's shooter.

"Oh," Peachy says, "he's not going to want to hear that. He hates that shit."

Well, I can sympathize. The leader of Richmond's finest loves to call press conferences to announce the department's latest nab, and sometimes he calls them a wee bit too early, which leads to an egg facial.

Still, the truth will out. Or it will if you give it a little help.

"Tell him I'm getting ready to write a story about how Gatewood couldn't have done it."

That's a bit of a stretch, but it gets Peachy's attention.

"OK. Let me run it by him. Damn, Willie. You don't give us much of a break over here, do you?"

I remind her of how it was, and is, on the other side, something she experienced as our first African-American female cops reporter. Her memory just needs a little jogging.

"Message received," she says, "but it's still not going to sit well with the chief."

I remind her that it's not my job to please L. D. Jones. I also ask her if she can check and see who, if anyone, Gatewood has called while he's been locked up. She asks me why and I say I can't tell her, other than it's not for publication in the newspaper.

"Anyhow," she says, lowering her voice and shifting gears, "when are you going to stop by for a little nip? Haven't seen you in a while."

Peachy Love is a fine woman, and we've shared the sheets on occasion. We probably will again, if Mr. Johnson is willing, but not right now. I tell her I'm seeing someone at the moment.

"Seeing someone? Like going steady? Are you going to ask her to the prom?"

"You seem amused."

"Well, I'm just goin' on history here."

I'm reminded of what Jumpin' Jimmy Deacon said the other night, when we were watching the Squirrels' home opener. The Curve had a leadoff hitter who managed to get himself picked off first base twice in one three-inning stretch.

Jimmy, ever the philosopher, shook his head.

"Those that's too dumb for history are condemned to repeat themselves," he said.

Yeah, I know what Peachy's talking about. I do sometimes wonder if I'm condemned to repeat myself.

Still, as Peggy once said when the fifth or sixth surrogate parent of my action-packed childhood had moved in and then moved on, "You've got to try or die."

Peachy calls me back thirty minutes later and says the chief will see me in an hour.

At two, I'm waiting in Jones's outer office. I think about how well we used to get along. We could have a drink or two, commiserate over lost wives and mourn simpler times.

Fate, though, has intervened. Because I've been involved in freeing a couple of people the Richmond police had already trotted before the cameras as "case closed," things are a little testier these days.

When I'm ushered in, he doesn't get up, doesn't even speak to me. After I've helped myself to the only chair in the room his butt's not occupying, he finally seems to notice my presence.

"What do you want?"

I explain, as succinctly as I can, about all those dead ex-ballplayers, taken before their time in a variety of manners, some mildly suspicious. I don't mention the threatening phone call Finlay Rand got. I'll wait for Peachy to check that one out, plus I want to talk to Gatewood himself.

If I was expecting L. D. to jump up and pin a citizen-helper award on me or make me an honorary member of the Richmond police department, I am bitterly disappointed.

"So what?" is Chief Jones's assessment of my accumulated knowledge. "So a bunch of old ballplayers died. Some of them were close to a natural death anyhow. Didn't one of them have a heart attack? And the one out hiking, he could've had one, too."

I mention the scorecards that several of the survivors remembered, with some of the numbers marked out.

"There's nothing left but the 2 and the 9," I tell him, "and somebody tried to kill Les Hacker."

"Who gives a shit?" Jones says. "You probably planted the idea of those numbers in their minds. Power of suggestion. I mean, c'mon. Some old baseball players died, some of them more than twenty years apart, and then somebody shot this Hacker guy. And we've got a nut case in lockup, guy with a record long as my dick, who was wearing the same jacket as the guy who did the shooting. And he had the key to the apartment he used in the coat pocket."

"He never shot anybody before, outside of Sandland."

L. D. shrugs.

"First time for everything. And he's killed plenty of people, I hear."

He stands, which I suppose is my cue to get the fuck out of there.

"You know," the chief says, "I feel kind of bad about it. I mean, he's obviously had his head messed with a little, over there doing his duty, killing Al Qaedas and shit, but we can't have a man just going around shooting the citizens."

He offers his hand, and I take it.

"I still think you've got the wrong guy," I tell him.

"Well," he says, "then show me the right guy. Don't come in here with some kind of Perry Mason bullshit. It's been my experience that the most logical answer is the right one. And Raymond Gatewood is the answer."

Not much else to say. I don't really blame L. D. His detectives came up with the obvious perp, and he's backing them up. Unfortunately, I think he is, not for the first time, putting his money on a losing horse.

BACK AT the car, I call Marcus Green's office. To my surprise, the great man himself answers.

"Things must be tough," I tell him. "Did you have to lay off your secretary?"

"They're called office managers. And I can still buy your ass and make you my lawn jockey. Kelly's taking a half day off."

"I wanted to talk about your client."

"Gatewood? What do you want to do, strangle him? Kate said the guy he allegedly shot was part of your, er, extended family."

I explain that I might have some information that could prove beneficial. I try to give Marcus the benefit of the doubt.

He's irritating as hell, but some people, for some reason, say the same thing about me. And despite the fact that he's got more than a little ambulance chaser in his blood, he's been known to defend the little guy. That's why Kate quit her job with an established law firm that has a money pit in the basement to work for or with him. And Marcus Green is no racist. Hell, Raymond Gatewood looks like the skinhead poster boy. Marcus's last name sums up his allegiance, color-wise. And he's smart enough to know you can't buy the kind of publicity you get when you play the white (or in Marcus's case, black) knight riding in to save the innocent victim. Pro bono, my ass.

All of Marcus's clients haven't been innocent, and I suspect he's gotten more than a few guilty ones off. But that just makes him more attractive to the well-heeled criminal class.

Yes, I tell him, Les Hacker is my mother's special friend, but that's not why I want to talk to Gatewood.

"I'm not even sure he's the shooter."

"Hell, the only people who are sure he's the shooter are the city cops."

I tell him that I'm working on more than a hunch.

"Tell me more," Green says.

"On the way to talk to your client, I'll fill you in. Pick me up at Perly's in an hour."

"Hour and a half," he says. "I'll bring your ex-wife along, too."

"Which one?"

Marcus's laugh, rich as mahogany, is almost enough to make him worth knowing.

I have time for a couple of Camels, a burger and fries and two Millers. I'm having the last one on the street when Marcus rolls up, five minutes late.

"Your driver off, too?" I ask, nodding to Kate in the front seat beside him.

"Yeah. You want a job? I hear you're taking a little time off."

"Just until I finish doing your job for you."

"You go to law school while I wasn't looking?"

I explain that I've figured out that his client almost certainly didn't try to kill Les. And then I explain, chapter and verse, what I've learned. I also tell them how little respect my theory has been given by L. D. Jones.

"L. D.'s a shithead," is Marcus Green's analysis.

We've been parked outside the jail for ten minutes by the time I finish my litany of the 1964 Richmond Vees' unhappy endings.

Then I tell Marcus and Kate about the little fly in Raymond Gatewood's ointment.

"This guy says one of Gatewood's friends called him and threatened him?" Kate says.

"That's what he says."

"I don't know," Kate says. "I don't have the impression he has many, if any, friends. And the ones he does have, they might not know how to use a telephone."

Marcus cuts the engine.

"Well," he says, "let's go find out."

I help Kate out of the car and wonder out loud when she's going to go on leave.

"Oh, I don't know," she says. "Maybe late September, or when my water breaks. What's it to you?"

She apologizes for being a little snippy. I tell her she looks great, which is mostly true.

It's been a long time since I've been around a pregnant woman full time, but my memories of Jeanette when she was carrying Andi almost make me feel sorry for Mr. Ellis. Almost. Kate's always been prone to get a little cranky when things weren't going the smooth way she had scripted them. No showing up late for appointments, no leaving dirty dishes on the table. No little buggers kicking around inside you and insisting on a timetable of their own.

GATEWOOD'S MENTAL health doesn't seem to have improved behind bars. He looks like he hasn't been sleeping much, and he's kind of twitchy.

After we listen to his litany of complaints about the food, the bed, the toilets and the lack of air conditioning, I ask him if he has any friends who might want to call Finlay Rand and rattle his fur-lined cage.

"Rand? Who the hell is Rand?"

"The guy whose condo they say you broke into," Marcus explains.

Gatewood just stares at us like we're speaking Urdu.

"No, man," he says at last. "I ain't got any friends. I got a damn brother that threw me out of his house. I got an ex-girlfriend that says she'll stick an ice pick in me if I ever try to see her again. The guys over there, they were my friends. Half of them are dead, and I don't know where the other fuckin' half are. Probably as messed up as me."

I've checked on that already, and he seems to be telling the truth about his lack of human contact. He claims to have nothing but contempt for his fellow street dwellers, and I believe him.

"This guy might have some good news for us, for you," Marcus says.

Gatewood scratches his head and complains that he thinks the jail has bedbugs, too.

"I could use a little good news."

I tell him about how all these old ballplayers have died, mostly before their time. I explain that Les Hacker was a teammate of theirs, one of two who haven't left this mortal coil, unless Rabbit Larue comes bounding out of the brush in the Georgia foothills one day asking what's for supper.

"So, you think somebody's killing a bunch of old ballplayers? What the hell for?"

I tell him I don't know, but if it means somebody other than him might have to take the rap for shooting Les Hacker, he might look on it as good news.

I ask him if he's made any phone calls.

"Other than to him?" He points at Marcus. "Nah. I haven't talked to anybody but him and her." He points to Kate.

"Well," I say, "if you do happen to remember a friend who might want to try to do you a favor by intimidating a witness, you might want to tell him to stop."

Gatewood fixes his thousand-yard stare on me.

"I already told you I don't have any damn friends. And I already told you I haven't called anybody. I don't lie, buddy."

Marcus puts on his best Mr. T frown and rubs his bald, shiny head like he's polishing a doorknob.

"We're not saying you do," he says, "but we have to make sure. We don't know you. Listen, I represent liars and thieves all the time. We have to make sure you're not covering up something. I don't plan to go before some jury and have the prosecutor spring something on me you should have already told me about."

"I told you the truth," Gatewood says.

Marcus Green closes his briefcase and stands up.

"Well," he says, "then our work here is finished. You might want to thank this fella here. If you get out of this mess, he's the one who's most responsible."

Gatewood looks at me. He doesn't appear to be grateful.

"He's just trying to get a story," he says and then turns his back on all of us, obviously tired of our company. I get the impression that Raymond Gatewood is not going to be a happy man even if we're able to get the police to drop charges. The happy train left the station a long time ago, when he was over there doing the president's work in Iraq and Afghanistan. We can help him with the life and liberty part, but I'm not sure the man waiting to go back to his cell even has the right shoes to pursue happiness anymore. Still, it's worth going after the truth, even if it sometimes seems like nothing but self-gratification, a hobby like stamp collecting. You've got to try or die.

Marcus looks at me and Kate. Time to go.

"WHAT DO you think?" I ask Marcus when we're outside.

He shrugs.

"I always believe my clients," he says, "until I don't believe them anymore."

I tell him that I'm going down to North Carolina to see the other surviving member of the '64 starting lineup.

"Are you going to be taking your little assistant with you?" Kate asks.

"Probably," I tell her. "What's it to you?"

Chapter Thirteen

Tuesday

*P*eachy Love calls me sometime after eight to tell me that Raymond Gatewood is telling the truth—at least about who he's telephoned. Two calls to Marcus Green's number, and that's it. He didn't even try to get in touch with anyone when they first bagged him, just waited for them to appoint an attorney. Marcus beat him to it, though, seeing a chance to show the world what a brilliant attorney he is. He grabbed the case before the judge could stick Gatewood with some rookie freebie.

"Well," Custalow says, "that's something anyhow. But Rand really seems spooked about something. He was asking me about it when I saw him in the lobby yesterday. He said to tell you he'd gotten another call."

As one of the Prestwould's two custodians, Abe Custalow sees more of this place than I do. People tend to like to talk to him, probably because he listens. He is my oldest friend in the world, next to my dear old mom. I imagine he can relate somewhat to Raymond Gatewood, having been a marine and a homeless person, and having an intimate relationship with our nation's penal system, thanks to a homicide that a judge decided wasn't quite justified enough to set Abe free. Finding him living in the park, right under my nose, was semiheartbreaking, and the good he does me by living here goes way beyond paying enough rent to keep Kate from evicting me from what is, technically, her condo. As was the case when we were kids, he often cleans up my mess, which can be considerable.

I talk with Peggy. Andi's going to take her over to see Les today. I promise her I'll be home by tomorrow noon at the latest and will stop by the hospital. Les is no better, but no worse. Peggy says they're trying to get him up to do some therapy, but he doesn't want to get out of bed.

"He says he's tired."

I promise her I'll give him a pep talk tomorrow. My problem with that pep talk is going to be that I keep imagining myself in Les's sad situation. I'd be telling anyone in charge of pep talks to go fuck themselves.

Cindy is there by nine, and we're on our way, on the last day for which the paper will actually pay for my little sabbatical.

Compared with a trip down I-95 south from Richmond, watching paint dry is exhilarating. Other than the occasional bonehead who thinks "95" also is the speed limit, there's not much to do except judge the relative tackiness of the signs leading to South of the Border—the combination gift shop, rest stop, amusement park and effrontery to Hispanic people everywhere that sits at the North Carolina-South Carolina state line.

When I tell Cindy we won't be going quite that far, she does a good job of hiding her disappointment.

We stop at the barbecue place Bootie Carmichael told me about, an hour north of our destination. Tragically, it does not serve beer, but the 'cue's OK. We have it with sweet tea, which is the only kind of tea there is south of Petersburg.

The turnoff to Buck McRae's place is just short of Fayetteville. We travel down a humpbacked county road with asphalt chipping off the sides for about three miles until I see the mailbox with "McRae" and a five-digit number on it. Actually, there are five boxes on the same post.

We drive for a quarter mile down a rut road, past a couple of kids who stop chasing each other with sticks long enough to stop and scowl at us. There are two houses off to the left and what appear to be at least four modular homes, a.k.a. trailers, downhill from the rise the second house is on.

My hunch is that Buck McRae, family patriarch, lives in the big house. No one answers when we knock at the front door, but when we go around back, a small African-American woman who appears to be in at least her seventies comes out on the screen porch. She has a pistol in her hand.

"Can I help you?" she says. Her upright posture and hard eyes tell me she's willing to do just about anything that needs doing, from feeding us to shooting us.

I explain who we are and why we're there.

"He's out there in the car house," she says, "trying to get that damn Buick to run."

She puts away her sidearm, to my relief, and we follow her.

"Buck!" she calls when we're still fifty feet away from the garage. "You got company. Get your ass over here."

She turns to us.

"I'm Lydia. You all want some iced tea?"

Buck McRae comes out from under the hood of a car whose main color is rust. He's rubbing his head.

"Got damn, woman," he says. "Don't scare me like that when I'm working."

She laughs. "You ain't working. You playing with cars."

He shakes his head.

"What you all want?"

Cindy walks back toward the house with Lydia, striking up a conversation like she's known her for years and Lydia wasn't holding a pistol a few minutes ago.

I tell Buck I'm the one who called about doing a story on the 1964 Richmond Vees. He frowns and doesn't say anything.

Buck McRae is as weathered as the Buick. His creases have creases. I can tell he's one of those guys who can't sit still, who isn't happy inside a house. He has fifty acres, he tells me. The four trailers belong to three of his children and one of his grandchildren. The little house next door, the only other one on the property that didn't come in on a truck, belongs to his brother.

"He's right poorly," Buck says. "He's gettin' old."

I know that Buck McRae never got beyond Triple-A ball, and that he retired in 1968, when he was just thirty-three, so I suppose he's seventy-seven now.

"I loved it," he says. "Loved playing ball. But we already had three kids by then, and I had to make a living."

He says he drove long-haul trucks for twenty years, leaving Lydia for as much as a week at a time to raise the kids. They bought the place where he lives now from a white family after the parents died and their offspring didn't care for the joys of country living.

"The kids and all just kind of followed us here," he says. "They get on your nerves sometimes, you know, but they're family."

He remembers most of the members of the '64 Vees.

"I hadn't kept in touch, though," he says. "We kind of went our own ways, you know."

I know McRae was the only black man on the team. I resist the urge to ask him things I already know the answers to, like how was it being a black man wearing a pro baseball uniform on a white team in Richmond, Virginia, in 1964. It's a lot better if people tell you things like that on their own. They don't think you're quite so stupid.

His memories of Les are good. He says he was the one guy on the team who treated him "like I was white." I ask him how close he came to making it to the big leagues. He shakes his head and frowns.

"I was good enough," he says, "but I got this reputation, you know."

I wait for it.

"I didn't take any crap. Or enough, anyhow, to suit some. There was a fight outside a restaurant some of us went to one night. Guy called me a nigger. I had to fuck him up, excuse my language. Black guy got arrested back then, there wasn't but one side to the story, and it wasn't his."

"They sent you down to Double-A."

"Yeah, after I hit .295 with nineteen home runs. I tore up the Southern League the next year, too. Know what that got me? Another year in Double-A."

He leans against a sawhorse that sits on the empty side of the two-car garage.

Finally, I get around to asking him if he can remember anyone trying to kill him.

He gives me the kind of look a question like that deserves. I give him the short version of what's happened to his Vees teammates over the years.

Buck shakes his head.

"Damn," he says. "What the hell for? I know people that don't like the Yankees, but that's ridiculous."

I tell him I'm as mystified as he is.

He gets up and walks around a little, going in circles on the dirt floor.

"Yeah," he says after a minute or so. "I think I know what you mean. It was eight years ago. Eight years ago this October, because I got out of the hospital right before Thanksgiving. Fella really messed me up good. We all figured he was high on crack or something. Wasn't any other way to explain it."

It turns out that Buck McRae, even in his seventies, drinks a bit "even though Lydia thinks I'm goin' to hell for it. And I have cut down some, since the shooting."

He says he went, as was his custom, to his favorite nip joint that night, a few miles up the road.

"The kind of place where, you know, like in that 'Cheers' show, everybody knows your name."

He says he remembers coming back to his car sometime after three.

"The place doesn't exactly have any closing hours," Buck explains. "Buddy just opens up when somebody wants a taste. But he doesn't allow no drugs or anything like that.

"I got in my truck, and while I'm sitting there, trying to remember where I hid my keys, this fella comes up and taps on my window. Like to have scared me to death. He had a mask on, but I could see his hands. He was white."

Buck stops walking and leans back against the Buick.

"He told me to get out of the truck. He had a big old pistol, stuck right in my face. I thought about blowing the horn, but there wasn't many people left inside by that time, and there wasn't any outside."

Buck says the man walked him over toward "the ditch," which turns out to be a drainage ditch, all that keeps the area around where Buck lives from turning into a swamp.

"He walked me maybe a hundred feet behind Buddy's, and then he told me to stop. He didn't even ask for money," Buck says, "although I sure was offering him some. He didn't say much, other than to tell me to shut the fuck up every now and then.

"I remember looking up there at this quarter moon goin' down off across the field, and thinking it might be the last thing I was ever gonna see."

What saved him, he says, was the ditch.

"It ain't but about five feet wide, but I guess that fella thought an old geezer like me couldn't jump across it. Maybe, if I didn't think I had to do it or die, I couldn't have. Amazin' what you can do when you have to."

Buck figures the man meant to back him up to the ditch, shoot him and leave him there for the buzzards to find in the next day or two.

"I figure he thought, with him and his big old gun behind me and the ditch in front of me, my options were kind of limited. He must of dropped his pistol for a second or two. If he'd had it trained on me, there ain't no way he could have missed."

Buck says he took three steps, screaming like a banshee, and leaped.

"I ain't one to go down easy."

He heard the first shot while he was in midair. The second one got him in the back.

"Just missed my spine, the doctor said."

There was a cornfield on the other side, and the farmer who owned it had never bothered to plow it under or burn it off that fall.

"I got in that corn, and there wasn't no way he was going to catch me," Buck says. "I don't think that fella could have jumped that ditch anyhow. He sounded like he was way past grown. And he was white. No offense."

He looks at me a little funny when he says that.

"I bet you could of jumped it, though."

I nod and he laughs, then continues.

"Of course, I was bleeding right much by then, and I reckon I passed out for a little bit. When I come to, it was quiet. I couldn't see my watch, but the moon was down, so I know it must have been sometime after five."

He managed to crawl back to the edge of the clearing, down near the building where he'd been drinking. By then, his eyes had adjusted enough to the dark that he could see across the ditch and could tell that there weren't any cars or trucks left in the parking lot.

"I yelled as loud as I could, but I was pretty weak by then. Finally, I got the dogs roused up, and then Buddy come out the front door, and he saw me across the ditch. The ditch was too wide for them to get a stretcher and me across it, and it took 'em to almost dawn to get an ambulance over there in that cornfield."

He had a punctured lung and had lost a lot of blood.

"Still paying off those hospital bills."

They never found the shooter. A man who'd left the nip joint twenty minutes before Buck came out said he'd seen a big truck, red, maybe a Ford, over in the corner of the parking lot, and a couple of men inside said they heard a truck drive off. From the time they gave, it was not long after Buck was shot.

"With the music and all, I don't reckon they heard the gun or me screaming."

They found a slug from a .45 and some footprints in the mud, but that was all they ever found.

"The NAACP wanted to get on it as a hate crime," Buck says. "I wouldn't have none of that. That fella was just out to kill somebody, regardless of race, creed or national origin."

He stops and lifts his shirt and undershirt. There's a star-shaped scar on his right side, purple against the backdrop of his light brown skin.

"Went right through," he says. "That fella wasn't into injuring or sending a message. He meant to kill me."

He pauses.

"And now, I guess I know what it was all about. Except I don't."

Me either, I tell him, but I intend to find out.

I ask him about the cards.

"Like with numbers and all?" he says. "Yeah. I got one not long after the accident, like what you're talking about, with numbers crossed out on it. It kind of rung a bell, because I'd got some other ones like that, years before. And then I got another one, maybe four years ago."

"Do you remember what the one after the accident looked like? I mean, what numbers were crossed out?"

"Hell, I don't remember that far back," he says. Then, after a pause, he says, "But I do have the one from four years ago."

I ask him if he thinks he could find it. He turns and walks toward the house, with me in tow.

Lydia and Cindy are chatting away like old friends on the big back porch. Buck tells me to sit and disappears into the old farmhouse. I accept Lydia's offer of sweet tea. She likes to cut to the chase, I soon discover.

"Where'd you get that nice tan?" It's clear she's not talking about anything I picked up at the beach or a salon. I give her the short version of my family history, including my long-gone, never-there father, Artie Lee.

"Well," she says, "you probably can pass with most folks. That's a blessing."

Buck comes out in five minutes with the card.

There are, as I would have guessed, nine numbers, with seven of them scratched off.

"The one I got in the hospital," he says, "I think it was like this one, but I think there was a question mark by the nine. The earlier ones, I can't remember much about them."

"If you hadn't of been drinking, none of this would of happened," Lydia reminds him, not, I'm sure, for the first time.

Buck laughs.

"I read the other day where a fella was walking along the beach somewhere up in Maryland, and this cliff alongside the beach just collapsed. Buried him alive on the spot. Maybe we oughta stop goin' to the beach, too."

"Maybe we ought to," Lydia says, getting up to refill our glasses.

I look at the card's postmark. El Dorado Hills, California.

I can tell that Buck doesn't want to talk about this any more in front of his wife. He motions for me to follow him back outside. I tell Cindy we won't be long. She tells me not to worry, that she's having a great time, as long as we're not taking Lydia and Buck away from something they need to do.

"That's the beauty of bein' old," Lydia says. "I don't need to do much. The kids and grandkids keep the house clean and the yard mowed. All we have to do is eat, sleep and watch the TV. The rest is optional."

We go back to the garage.

"So Les Hacker and me are the only ones still alive, and somebody's tried to get rid of both of us?"

I tell him that's the way it looks.

He nods his head.

"Two and nine," he says. "Catcher and right field. Don't know why I didn't figure that out before."

I tell him there wasn't much reason to suspect anything until now.

"You always have to expect stuff," he says. "Nothing is an accident. If I'm a little more careful, or a little less drunk, that fella doesn't sneak up on me in the parking lot. If he's a little more careful, I don't get a chance to jump that ditch.

"If somebody you don't know sends you a postcard with a bunch of numbers on it, they mean something. If you get careless and ignore 'em, you got nobody to blame but yourself."

I have the impression that Buck McRae is the kind of man who takes responsibility for whatever happens, even if he can't stop it from happening.

"Satchel Paige was my hero, my idol, when I was growing up," he says. "He was forty-some years old when they finally let his black ass play in the big leagues, and he still stuck it up their butts.

"Satchel said not to look back, that something might be gaining on you. Well, I have to disagree with him on that one. You want to look back, because if you don't, whatever's gaining on you is gonna catch you and eat you."

I shake Buck McRae's hand, which is as tough and weathered as Les Hacker's old catcher's mitt that he keeps in the attic.

"You tell Les to hang in there," he says. "Tell him I'd like to see him again sometime. And, for God's sake, don't mention any of this to Lydia."

I tell Buck that I'll let him do the worrying for both of them. I also tell him that I doubt that whoever came after him eight years ago will try again. We both know that might be wishful thinking, though.

IT'S LATER than I'd planned by the time we leave the McRaes' home, almost six thirty. Cindy accepts my suggestion that we get a hotel room and then some dinner.

We find a hotel for less than seventy bucks that doesn't seem to have bedbugs. The clerk suggests a place to get dinner a couple of miles toward town with an all-you-can-eat buffet.

I call Peggy on her cell.

"He won't eat, and he doesn't even try to talk anymore," she says. "Even Awesome can't get him to smile."

I tell her I'll be back tomorrow.

At the buffet, everything's been fried in the same grease, and the patrons look as if they've been coming here a long time. Some of them are so big that it's hard for two of them to pass each other in the buffet line.

I suggest a bar, and we find one in Fayetteville's downtown. Like a lot of towns, it's trying to bring back the fifties, before the department stores, movie theaters, clothing stores and every damn thing else fled to the suburbs. What you get, when you do that, is a lot of chi-chi restaurants, second-hand stores and government offices with apartments overhead. I wish them well, but it looks to me like the big spending still goes on out there in Bubbaland.

We have a couple of beers at a place with exposed brick and a small but enthusiastic crowd. After "a couple" turns into four or five, Cindy says she's tired. Hell, I say, I'm not tired, and I'm just getting into a very interesting conversation with a guy who looks like he spent a few years in the army about whether we should have invaded Iraq. I'm about to order another beer when I look at Cindy and can see the message, big as life, in her eyes. Last call. As in last call for this fine, sweet woman to make my life appreciably better.

You might think it's an easy enough thing to say, "Check, please," to a bartender. Maybe it is, for you.

On the way back to our room, not much is said.

When we get inside, Cindy pulls my head down and kisses me for a long time.

"Thank you," she says. "I appreciate the effort."

What I'm thinking, though, and maybe what she's thinking too, is: How many times will I be able to say "check, please"?

"What now?" she asks me later, as we're lying in a twist of sheets and bedspread. I'm not sure whether she's talking about me and her or about the 1964 Vees.

Because it's easier to talk about the second issue than the first, I tell her what's been on my mind for a few days now. "It's time to go find Frannie Fling."

Chapter Fourteen

WEDNESDAY

*P*eggy's spending a lot of her time on the cot in Les's room. I drive over as soon we get back and I have time to drop Cindy off with a promise to call her in a few hours. I take Awesome Dude with me to the hospital. He's been more or less fending for himself and hasn't burned the house down yet, although the strong scent of burned popcorn indicates that perhaps Awesome hasn't had too much experience with microwaves.

"He's gonna pull through," Awesome says when we're getting out of the car. "I know he is. Les, he's tough."

I give Awesome a little squeeze, which makes him jump a little. Even after being taken in by Peggy like a stray mutt and treated like family, he's still not cool with people invading his space. In the Dude's life, most people who have touched him have not meant him well.

Jumpin' Jimmy Deacon is there. I was hoping he would be. I need some information.

Les looks like he's lost twenty pounds in the last thirteen days. I sit beside him for a few minutes and try to engage him. When I tell him I've just been to see Buck McRae, his eyes light up, and I know he understands what I'm saying. Despite being shot and then having a stroke, and despite the fact that he wasn't clicking on all cylinders mentally before all this happened, Les is still with us. He can still pull 1964 out of his memory bank.

When I tell him Buck wants to come see him sometime soon, his mouth twists into something resembling a smile, and he shakes his head.

Peggy pulls me into the hallway to tell me that the hospital, having somehow let him have a major stroke on their watch and not noticing it in time to reverse its effects, now wants to kick Les out.

"They said they can't do anything else for him," my mother says, sniffling a little. "They say we need to find a nursing home or 'assisted care facility' or some damn thing."

I can tell she's overwhelmed. Hell, I'm overwhelmed. Most people don't deal with the inevitable until it's, well, inevitable. Who wants to sit down after dinner one night and come up with a plan for what to do when you're so bad off that the hospital says they can't help you?

I tell her we'll work through this. My first job will be to find out who exactly gave her Les's eviction notice. We need to talk.

After an hour or so, Jumpin' Jimmy says he's going outside. I say I'll go with him. On the trip to North Carolina, I tried to keep my nicotine intake to a minimum. I have this feeling that I'm running up a few demerits with the lovely Ms. Peroni, and she, like so many others in our intolerant world, has a bias against tobacco.

I need a smoke.

I also need to pump Jimmy Deacon.

"Jumpin' Jimmy's not feeling so good about old Les," he says when we're far enough away from the room. "Les, he was always a fighter, but . . ."

"Yeah."

When we get far enough away from the smoke police that I can fetch a Camel from my shirt pocket, I get to what's on my mind.

"I need to get in touch with Frannie Fling's family."

Jimmy frowns. He's thinking. I can smell something burning.

"She didn't have much family," he says. "By the time I got up there, when I went looking for her grave, they had moved."

"You say you thought they went to Massachusetts?"

"Something like that. What're you so interested for now?"

I tell him that, if I'm going to do the story I want to do about the 1964 Vees, I need to find out more about Frannie Fling.

"Well," he says, "just don't go making her look like she was some kind of whore or something. Jimmy would not like that."

His eyes are kind of red, and his fists are clenched.

I promise Jimmy that I will do right by Frances Flynn.

SARAH GOODNIGHT answers on the first ring. She says the latest rumor at the paper is that we won't be getting any raises again this year. *Quelle surprise.* I think this makes it four years in a row.

The newsroom has its own half-ass union that is about as worthless as a broke-dick dog when you really get down to dollars and cents. Being a union, and a pissant one at that, in a right-to-work state entitles you to complain a lot. When times were good, our management did not stint on paying the help. But we got spoiled, and when the big stores went out of business or just quit buying print ads, and the geniuses above us decided to give it away online, we found out an obvious (to everyone but us) fact of life: When rich people have to decide between taking care of their families or taking care of the help, the help bites the big one.

"Too bad my landlord decided to give himself a raise this year," Sarah says. "I'm losing money, Willie."

"Maybe they can dip into my pension fund and give you a taste."

She snorts.

"Pension! Like I'll ever see one."

I sympathize. Not enough to give up my pension until they tear it from my cold, dead hands, but I do wonder what's going to happen to Sarah and to Andi and everyone else who came up in this benighted century, when pensions are but a fond memory and the 401(k) plans that were supposed to replace them aren't being funded any more.

Changing the subject, I ask her how things are going on night cops.

"I hope to hell you're through playing sportswriter soon," she says.

I tell her that it won't be long, especially since now I'm dipping into my paid vacation time to fund my little junket.

"Last night," she says, "I had to go to your old neighborhood."

"Oregon Hill?"

"Yeah. It was a real mess. Somebody tried to jack a guy's car, right there on Pine Street."

I'm a little surprised. Crime in Richmond tends to restrict itself to certain neighborhoods: Poor sides of town (there's more than one), places where bars empty their little feuds into the street, the area around VCU, because students don't know enough to be scared and not walk their dogs at four A.M. Oregon Hill, though, usually doesn't have many dots on the crime map.

"Tell me more."

"Four idiots from Blackwell, I think it is, from the address, apparently jumped this guy, just as he was getting out of his car. But they didn't realize, I guess, that there were, like, three men sitting on the porch across the street, talking.

"They said the would-be victim almost beat one guy to death, and the guys from the porch gave the other three a pretty good pounding before they ran them off in the direction of Hollywood Cemetery. The cops caught up with them later. The guy they tried to jack was driving some kind of vintage car, a Corvette, I think. Said he used to be a boxer."

"The Corvette was red?"

"Yeah. I saw it."

"Walker Johnson."

"How the hell did you know that, Willie?"

Goat Johnson's brother was two years older than I was. It was the classic Hill family. Goat's the president of some half-ass college in Ohio. Walker was a professional boxer for a while before a romantic entanglement with cocaine led to his early retirement and a brief stint as a guest of the state. Bad man to mess around with, even if he's got to be almost fifty-five now.

When I was growing up, coming to Oregon Hill to prey on the citizens was like going into a lion's cage to steal his dinner. It's good to know that, even with the current gentrification, some things haven't changed.

"They're talking about charging the guy with attempted murder."

"With his fists?"

"Well, he was a boxer."

What a bunch of bullshit. I hope sanity prevails. It's depressing sometimes how seldom that happens, though. The little punk will probably sue him.

I tell Sarah to hang on for a few more days and ask her to transfer me to Ed Chenowith.

"Another favor?" he says, sounding like his dance card is pretty much full.

"How'd you know?"

"Nobody calls unless they want something."

I bring up old times.

"Yeah, yeah. You're right. You're not a complete asshole. What do you need?"

It's about as close to a compliment as Chenowith offers these days. As with a lot of his newsroom compatriots, much of his good will disappeared at about the same time that his raises and matching 401(k) contributions stopped and his pension was frozen. Why can't people eat shit gracefully?

I tell him that I'm trying to track down Frances Flynn's relatives, if there are any. All I know from Jumpin' Jimmy is that everybody had left by the time he visited her grave and that they were supposed to have moved to Massachusetts. And Jimmy remembered her parents' names, William and Eleanor.

"That's about all I know, though. She might have had some other family, maybe siblings."

I tell Chenowith a little of the story, just enough to get his juices flowing. I know he's addicted to research and won't be able to stop until he finds Frances Flynn's family, if there's any of it left.

I lay a big smooch on Ed's ass. He says he'll call me when he has something.

I go back into the hospital and, after many false starts, get in touch with the person who can try to explain to me how Les Hacker should be kicked out of the hospital.

"We just can't do anything else for him," the woman says. She's about half my age and has that same empathy for the human condition as the average human resources drone.

I point out to her that he had a stroke on their watch, or un-watch as it turns out.

"Well," she says, "according to my information, he was on around-the-clock surveillance. Sometimes, these things just happen."

When I note that this is a piss-poor way for a hospital to explain ruining what's left of a man's life, she closes her little folder and suggests that the decision has already been made, that she's sorry and that there's nothing that can be done.

I suggest that there sure as shit is something that can be done, but I'm going to have to hire a lawyer to do it.

She gives me a tired smile. I almost feel sorry for her. She's probably got a degree in history or psychology, and it's either this job or join Andi and her legion waiting tables.

"I'm sorry," she says.

Not much else to do but leave.

On the way back home, I take a left on Fifth Street, just for the hell of it. The empty parking space right beside Penny Lane is an obvious sign I'd be foolish to ignore. I pull in and walk in. I have a light supper of fish and chips and three Harps. Better to keep dinner simple at Penny Lane. "English" and "cuisine" are two words that do not often go well together.

While I'm standing in the men's room, contemplating a fourth Harp and whatever follows that, my phone rings. It slips from my hand, and only the kind of reflex action common to great athletes and drunks lets me catch it in midair before I piss all over it.

It's Ed Chenowith.

"I think I have something for you," he says. It's been less than four hours since we talked. I compliment him on his fast work.

"The father is dead," he says. "Died a year after his daughter. The mother married again, a guy named Roger Fairchild. They settled in Worcester, Massachusetts."

"Do you have an address?"

"She died, too, last year. And she outlived her second husband, too."

"So, dead end."

"Not exactly."

Chenowith has knocked himself out. He's gone that extra mile and found out that Eleanor Harshman Flynn Fairchild had, in addition to two kids from her second marriage, another son, Frances's younger brother. Adair Flynn. Eleanor also had a brother, a little younger than her. He was born March 7, 1925, so he'd be eighty-seven years old now.

"And he's still alive. Still lives in Wells, too. I don't know if he's got all his marbles, but as of five days ago, he was still alive."

I get his name. August Harshman. And his address. Chenowith has his phone number, too. He doesn't seem to have e-mail. Probably doesn't tweet, either.

"I owe you about a case of Early Times," I tell Ed.

"You can't do better than that?" he says, and hangs up.

I zip up, make my way out of the world's smallest bathroom, pay my tab and leave. The scent of a good story is just about the only thing that can get me to quit after just a few. Well, maybe that and Cindy Peroni.

I stop by the paper, go online and find Wells, Vermont. It's not that far from Albany, where I'm told planes take off and land on a regular basis. I call Cindy and ask if it would be possible to impose on her good will for one more little junket. She says she has classes tomorrow that she can't miss. She's already bagged too many following me to exotic places like Tallahassee and Fayetteville.

"But let me see what I can do," she says.

She calls me back and tells me that she's gotten her brother to pull some strings, and I'll be on a very cheap flight to Albany, New York.

Cindy seems impressed that I am in my own abode not long after nine P.M.

"I thought you might call a little earlier," she says. I explain that between trying to keep Les from being thrown out of the hospital and trying to find the dregs of Frannie Fling's family, I've been a little busy. I realize that the lovely Cindy Peroni, who must have much better prospects than me on her social calendar, has probably blown her evening waiting to hear from me.

I promise to do better. Promising to do better is one of the things I do best.

Chapter Fifteen

THURSDAY

*T*he seven fifteen A.M. flight to Albany seems like cruel and unusual punishment for a man who cut his evening short by a good three hours in order to embark on what stands a good chance of being a wild goose chase.

I get to the airport by five thirty and barely make my plane. I look down, as I'm in my seat, and realize I've left my belt in the plastic tray where I deposited it and pretty much everything else on my person to appease the smiling, friendly security folks. Ah, well. They probably sell belts at the Albany airport. Then, having hurried up, we wait. Somebody sneezes in Chicago and the whole aviation system loses two hours. But flying beltless and late beats the hell out of driving all the way to Wells, Vermont.

We land before noon, even with the change in Newark, and my rental car and I are on the road, headed east.

I CALLED August Harshman last night. On about the sixth ring, someone picked up.

"Yes," he said. "What is it? Whatever you've got, I don't want any."

I assure Mr. Harshman, who sounds hale enough to be irritable, that I am not a telemarketer. I tell him about my story, on a minor-league baseball team nearly fifty years in the rearview mirror.

"I was told that your niece, Frances Fling, er, Flynn, was friends with one of the players on that team who is now deceased."

There is a long silence.

"You know that my niece is long since dead, I presume."

I tell him that I do. I have the feeling that he's about to lump me with the solicitors for the Deputy Sheriff's Benevolent Society and hang up.

"But a man who worked for the team back then told me what a wonderful girl she was, and I wanted to hear more about her, for the story."

Maybe he knows I'm blowing smoke up his ass. Maybe he just wants to get me off the phone but doesn't want to hang up on me. Finally, he agrees that, if I come by tomorrow, he thinks he can find a few minutes to talk to me about his late sister's late daughter.

It would have been impolite, to say nothing of stupid, to wonder out loud why an eighty-seven-year-old man is so pressed for time that he can only spare a few minutes. But if he knew me, he'd know I'm like cockroaches. Once you let me in the door, it's damn hard to get rid of me.

I FIND the house on only the third drive through Wells. The locals give me directions that seem to presume that I know the names of every person and identity of every tree and bush in the neighborhood.

I stop a man walking to his car from the hardware store. He describes a route that seemingly would take me through the majority of the New England states. When I point out that, according to my map, the Harshman estate seems to be some-where on the gravel road somewhere up ahead, he throws his hands in the air and says, "Well, go that way then, if you want to!"

Finally, on that gravel road within eyesight of such Wells, Vermont, as there is, I see the mailbox, half-hidden by a rose bush, with "Harshman" painted on the side.

August Harshman's house is halfway up a sizable hill. I cross a bridge over a creek that seems to be about one thunderstorm short of overflowing. The house, a wooden Victorian, faces west, and the view of the mountains makes me wonder what housing prices are like up here.

I knock and, after a minute or so, I can hear a faint tapping that grows louder. Finally, the door opens.

"You're late," August Harshman says, leaning on his cane. He turns his back to me, and I follow him, very slowly, inside. He's a tall man, still over six feet despite what I assume is some octogenarian shrinkage. He's thin, and I sense that he's always been thin. An old dog of mixed ancestry with a suspicion of strangers looks up from the wooden floor with yellow, baleful eyes. When he tries to bark, he sounds as old as Harshman. Harshman tells him to hush, and he does. A small and welcome fire crackles.

He offers me nothing. When he sits, in a Barcalounger that has adjusted to his contour and absorbed his smell, I take the next-most-comfortable option, a straight-backed wooden dining-room chair. It is a poor second, but at least I'm in the door, talking to Frannie Fling's nearest living relative that I'm able to track down.

I ask Harshman if he lives there alone. He says he has a daughter who lives in San Francisco.

"She comes to see me twice a year," he says, "and she doesn't want to do that. I can tell."

Have you thought, I want to ask him, about buying her a more comfortable second chair? Might make a difference.

He does allow, though, that his daughter would like him to move out west with her.

"So she can take care of me," he says, spitting it out like she'd cursed him. "I won't do it, though. They'll never get me west of the Hudson, I can tell you that."

I let him talk awhile. I thought New Englanders were supposed to be a close-mouthed bunch, lots of ay-ups followed by long silences. I certainly would have expected that of August Harshman. Like a lot of tight-lipped people, though, once you get him going, he's like the damn Energizer Bunny. Just keeps going and going.

His sister, he says, married beneath her. The Flynns were "shanty Irish," but the late Eleanor was taken by Willie Flynn's charm and good looks, "so-called."

"Frannie, she was beautiful," he says, his tone softening. "She had that wild streak, though, just like her father. Willie drank, you know. Grown man named Willie, not William or Bill, you had to know he was the irresponsible type. No offense."

I opt not to tell Mr. Harshman that Willie's my given name. It would just get in the way of the information, which is what I'm here for.

I spend a couple of hours with August Harshman, and he tells me as much as anyone living could about Frances Flynn.

She was, as I've already been told by Jumpin' Jimmy Deacon, a good student who decided that her future did not include Wells, Vermont.

"They would have sent her to college," Harshman says. "Mary and I had offered to help, but not long after that, she ran away."

The Flynns didn't hear from their daughter for some months.

"She had done some things that didn't set well with her parents, or at least with Eleanor, and I think there had been a falling out."

By the time Frannie came back to Wells with her tail between her legs, it soon became obvious that she was pregnant.

"Eleanor was funny," Harshman says. "She married this fella who was about two steps up from the town drunk, but she had this moral side. Maybe she just wanted Frannie to have a better life than she'd had.

"We tried to stop her from kicking Frannie out, and I know Willie was against it. But Eleanor ran that house. She controlled everything except Willie's drinking. Nobody could control that."

And so Frannie went to live in the home of a friend whose parents weren't quite as judgmental.

"And then, that spring, we heard she was gone again, back down south."

When notified of Frannie's death, Eleanor Flynn went from hard-hearted mother to avenging angel. She threatened a lawsuit and more or less called down the wrath of God on the New York Yankees.

"Nineteen sixty-five, that was a sad year," Harshman says as he gets up to stoke the fire and put another couple of pieces of wood on it. The dog follows him with his eyes wherever he goes.

"We lost Frannie in March, and then Willie . . . well, I think it killed him. He'd never needed much of an excuse to drink, and now he had every reason in the world to try to drink the world dry."

Willie Flynn died that November. They found his frozen body by the same creek I drove over on the way to Harshman's house. His widow was so angry at him that she had him cremated and his ashes thrown away, Harshman says.

"He should have been stronger. If nothing else, he should have thought about the boy."

"The boy?"

He looks at me like I'm slow. Maybe it's my southern accent.

"Her brother. Dairy. He was the only one they had left, and instead of getting closer to him, holding him tighter, they all just seemed to go their separate ways."

His name was Adair. Adair Enoch Flynn. Adair had been his father's mother's last name. Enoch was his mother's father's name. Hell of a moniker to put on a kid.

Dairy Flynn was eight years younger, so he was ten when Frannie went south the first time, eleven when she died.

"He was real fond of his big sister," Harshman says. "In some ways, I think it was worse on him than on Eleanor and

Willie. He kept a picture of her in his room until after she died and Eleanor came in one day and threw it away. They had a big fight over it, she told me. She said he came after her with a baseball bat. Willie had to take it away from him."

August Harshman sighs.

"You know," he says, "they were too hard on her. I heard about how she went back down there to get that fella, that ballplayer, to marry her. But I really think that, if they had took her in and accepted that girls do get that way sometimes, no matter how well you raise them, and offered to take care of that child like it was their own, she would have stayed up here and none of what happened would have happened.

"But it was 1964. You didn't get pregnant until you got married, although some did and just took care of things without a lot of fuss."

He says Eleanor told him once, many years later, that she would have given anything to have saved Frannie, if she had known how it was going to turn out.

"Didn't stop her from doing what she did about Dairy, though."

I think about Peggy, about how she must have felt, younger even than Frances Flynn, when her parents told her she had to leave with her bastard, mixed-race baby in tow. I am here either because Peggy was a stronger person than Frannie Flynn or because of plain damn good luck.

After Willie Flynn froze to death in the late fall of 1965, Eleanor moved with her son to Worcester, Massachusetts, where a cousin was able to get her a job as a secretary. Despite the fact that she was in her early forties, she was still apparently quite an attractive woman. Within two years, she had caught the eye of one of her bosses, Roger Fairchild, and within four years, he was divorced and they were married, in 1969.

It turned out, Harshman tells me, that Roger Fairchild wasn't really in the market for a package deal. He was more than happy to take the mother, but when it came to Dairy, it was "no sale."

"Dairy was kind of difficult. He got in some trouble down there in Worcester. Never did learn all about it. He'd come up here and stay with us for a week in the summer, and even that long, he could be a pill. Damn near burned the barn down last time he visited."

Roger and Eleanor Fairchild soon started a belated family of their own, adopting two kids. By the time Dairy turned eighteen, he was a high school dropout who was too old anymore for anyone to even try to control.

"They kicked him out. Just told him he'd have to live somewhere else. Eleanor told me later that Roger said it was either Dairy or him."

And so, for the second time in seven years, Eleanor evicted her own child. I'm wondering how the Fairchilds' two youngest children turned out.

When I hear all this crap, and I think about how Peggy took care of her own unforgiving mother in her later, helpless years, I want to take the next plane south and give my old dope-addled mom a very big hug.

"We kind of offered to let him stay here," Harshman says, but I can't imagine the offer was especially heartfelt, given Dairy's track record.

Instead, Harshman says Dairy stayed in Worcester, rooming with some friends, doing whatever work a high school dropout with an attitude problem could find.

"And then, he just disappeared."

His mother would try to keep in touch, which understandably wasn't easy. One day, Harshman says, she realized it had been eight months since anyone had seen him. His friends said they always figured he would come back. He had a tendency to disappear for weeks if not months on end, then come back with outrageous stories about adventures on fishing boats or scamming tourists out on Cape Cod.

The cops didn't seem to have much interest in finding him. Nobody had much interest, I'm thinking but not saying. After a while, everyone forgot about Dairy Flynn.

"Later on, Eleanor never wanted to talk about him. I tried a couple of times, but she'd just cut me off, say something like, 'we couldn't save him,' and the conversation would be closed."

He gets up once, to show me a photograph of Dairy Flynn, circa 1971. He looks a little like his sister. He also looks pissed off.

I see no sense in mentioning the fate of the 1964 Vees to August Harshman, other than to mention that most of them have gone on to their reward.

He gives me directions to the cemetery where Frances Flynn is buried.

"Oh," he says, as I'm leaving, "did you want something to drink. Some water, maybe, or coffee?"

I tell him no thanks, and not to bother to get up. I can let myself out. He and his dog are more than willing to take me up on that.

The cemetery is easier to find than Harshman's house was. Frannie's grave is a challenge, though. The graves aren't in any sort of order, not parallel or perpendicular to each other for the most part, just rambling all over the hill that overlooks the town.

Finally, I find it. Harshman said he hadn't been out to see her grave for a couple of years. "I go to enough funerals as it is without keeping up with all the already dead." But Frannie's grave looks better kept than most of the ones around it. There are no other Flynns residing here that I can see. I know from my afternoon interview that her father isn't buried anywhere, and that Eleanor is resting in peace back in Worcester.

Somebody, though, has sure as hell been here.

Frances Flynn's gravestone seems to be of the cut-rate variety, and it's adorned only by her name and dates of birth and death. On top of it, though, slowly wilting in the Vermont April that feels like Virginia February, are two dozen yellow roses.

I HAVE an eight P.M. flight back to Richmond, and it's four thirty already when I start toward Albany. I'm barely out of Wells when my cell phone goes off.

Just as I answer and determine that Jumpin' Jimmy Deacon is calling me, I drive into a deep, dark valley, and I lose the reception. I know my life has been changed in wondrous ways by the invention of the cell phone, but sometimes I just want to throw the damn thing out the window.

When I get to the top of the next hill, with a view of what must be the Adirondacks in front of me, I call back.

"Willie," the voice on the other end says, "Jumpin' Jimmy's got some real bad news. Les is gone."

Chapter Sixteen

FRIDAY

*L*es took his final turn for the worse about two yesterday afternoon, Peggy told me when I got back last night.

She, Awesome Dude and Jumpin' Jimmy were there. Les looked over at Peggy and squeezed her hand, and then he squeezed it harder, and then he let go.

This time, the hospital was a little more diligent about keeping an eye on him, or maybe it was just Peggy screaming at the top of her lungs that got help there in a hurry.

There wasn't much they could do, though. The hemorrhage probably would have taken out someone in much better shape than Les. They did all they could, wheeling him away to work their magic while others herded Peggy, Awesome and Jimmy to the "family room." A professional trained in delivering bad news came in shortly after three thirty and told them what they already knew.

"I wish I could have seen him one more time," Peggy said, knowing that the Les she loved for the last twelve years had left several days before they hauled his body away.

"We shoulda got married," she says. We're sitting in her living room and, yes, she's already had something to smoke, and it's not yet nine o'clock. Wanna make something of it? "He offered

---

EAST BATON ROUGE PARISH LIBRARY
Main Library

Borrowed on 08/18/2014 10:22 Till

1) Remains of innocence
   Due date: 09/29/2014
   No.: 31659040515716
2) The director : a novel
   Due date: 09/29/2014
   No.: 31659041051190
3) Parker Field : a Willie Black mystery
   Due date: 09/29/2014
   No.: 31659041527322

Total on loan : 5

To renew items call 225-231-3744
or visit www.ebrpl.com
08/18/2014 - 10:22

to, but I said I hadn't had very much luck with marriage, and he said whatever suited me, suited him."

By the time I got in last night, half of Oregon Hill was at Peggy's house. My mother won't have to cook for a year, if she can keep all this crap from spoiling. Nobody misses a death pageant up here, even if they haven't spoken to the deceased in ten years. Even Jerry Cannady, stepping briefly outside his pest persona, went down to KFC and brought a bucket of chicken to add to the redneck bacchanalia. People I hadn't seen in years were there. Walker Johnson very considerately brought a twelve-pack of Blue Ribbon with him. We toasted Les and I congratulated him on making bail.

"Goat posted it," he said. "I don't think he's too proud of me."

I told him that kicking the punk's ass was the honorable thing to do. He seemed pleased.

I sat with Peggy and then, with Cindy's help, started making all the arrangements nobody ever wants to make. I am thankful that Les didn't tell us he wanted his body shipped back to Wisconsin or frozen like Ted Williams's head. As was Les's custom, he kept it simple, doing what caused those around him the least trouble. He'd made it clear that a cremation was fine with him. Still, there were a thousand things to do, and we couldn't get Peggy to quit obsessing.

Cindy was already at my mother's house when I got there.

"Peggy," she said, putting her arm around her after she'd worried out loud for about the fifteenth time about finding a minister, "go smoke something. We've got this covered."

This morning, I have to face the abyss without the nervous energy that kept me going last night.

Now, it's just sad. I mean, I really am going to miss Les Hacker. I am not used to mourning the people who are really close to me. Sure, I've seen three wives come and go, but they're just not sharing my address. They're not gone for good, not gone-gone. When I was a kid, I saw father figures decide that they weren't really ready for commitment, then sat with Peggy when she told me, more than once, that it was just me and her, that we were well rid of the sons of bitches.

None of that prepares me for this. And my duty, as the secondary mourner, is to try to help Peggy get through it.

"What am I going to do?" she says. Her eyes are all puffy and she can't sit still.

I tell her that she'll do what she did before Les came along, which starts her crying again. Awesome Dude is shaking his head at me. My interpersonal skills apparently have sunk to subDude level.

I tell her that I will always be here. For better or worse, so does Awesome. But it sucks, without a doubt. Peggy has been as self-sufficient as anyone I've ever known. She raised a kid with a suspicious tan here in Alabaster Acres with damn little help from anyone, daring anybody to suggest she wasn't worthy of their respect.

"Sometimes," she told me once, after I'd been sent home from school again for fighting, "you've got to just keep hitting them until they respect you."

She carried her own weight and mine, somehow finding the money to send me to college. And then, when love or even endurable male companionship seemed to have grabbed the last train out of town, she met Les Hacker. Les brought a blessing and a curse with him. The blessing was that, for the first time since she was a teenager, she had someone she could lean on, 24-7. The curse? It couldn't last forever. Peggy let her guard down, let love and trust slip in the back door. Now, with Les gone, it's like taking a kid from an orphanage, letting her live with a big, happy family for a few years, and then sending her back.

It is not enough to suggest that my mother should be happy for the good times they had. That pearl of wisdom can wait for a time when common sense starts edging grief out the door.

Andi's here, too. She's been a rock for her grandmother the last two weeks. I ask her how she's able to get so much time off. She says there are a million restaurant jobs out there, and anyone who thinks she ought to put work before family can kiss her butt.

I tell my daughter that I don't know how she could have turned out so well, considering who her father is. She tells me to shut up.

In the early afternoon, I step outside on the porch to have a smoke.

My old buds are here. Abe's gotten off early from his custodial duties, and we're joined by R. P. McGonnigal and Andy Peroni. Andy, ever mindful of the solemnity of the occasion, asks me if I'm screwing his sister. I tell him to go inside and ask her himself.

"I can't believe you still smoke that shit," R. P. says. Hell, we all smoked when we were kids. It was the manly thing to do. Like underage drinking and getting arrested, it was part of the Hill rites of passage.

I tell him that I'm only doing it to keep my weight down.

"You oughta try it," I tell him, knowing that Richard Petty McGonnigal is as vain as a cheerleader about his appearance.

We tell the stories we always tell. Some of them never even happened, or at least not the way we remember them now. I know that Andy Peroni never pissed in the baptismal fount at the Baptist church just before a few sinners were saved one Sunday morning, but he always meant to, and that's practically the same thing. Our stories, like our waistlines, have evolved.

"Les was a prince," R. P. says, and we all nod.

"He's the only one Peggy never kicked to the curb," Custalow says. We agree that this is high praise indeed.

I've smoked my second Camel and am about to go back inside when Abe pulls me to the only corner of the porch that isn't awash with mourners.

"Rand was asking about you today," he says. "He said to tell you that he's gotten another call. Whoever's calling him seems to think that somehow Rand can get that guy out of jail by not pressing charges."

By this time, I'm about ready to let the world do what it will with Raymond Gatewood. I don't like the son of a bitch. But the evidence seems to be undeniable to just about anyone except our fine police chief that Gatewood isn't Les's shooter. Or, if he is, it's a hell of a coincidence, because somebody's been picking off the '64 Vees for about twenty-seven years. I'm pretty sure Raymond Gatewood wasn't killing people before he was toilet-trained.

"He says he's afraid to go outside."

"Well, Gatewood hasn't talked to anybody except me and his lawyers, unless he's got somebody in the lockup who's trying to do him a favor. And I tend to believe him when he says he doesn't have any friends. He's worked pretty hard at that."

I start to go inside again. The funeral's going to be on Monday, and I'm starting to feel like Peggy. We've got a hundred things to do. There are still cousins in Wisconsin who haven't been notified, although if they were close, I suppose one or more of them might have hauled their asses down here before Les died. I know Peggy got the word to what family Les had left up there.

"Wait," Custalow says, putting his hand on my arm. "There's something else."

Abe doesn't usually talk for the sake of talking. If he has "something else," it's probably worth my time to discover what it is.

"I found something," he says, "but I want to show it to you. It might be nothing, but you need to see it."

I promise Abe Custalow that, as soon as I can spare a few minutes from dealing with my mother's (and my) grief, he can show me what he's talking about.

Abe has to get back to the Prestwould. I hesitate for a moment, then pull out another Camel. I'm not quite ready to go back in there yet.

Chapter Seventeen

Saturday

Abe Custalow has, as has often been the case in our fucked-up, intertwined lives, shown me the light.

The first time I saw him, I think Abe was whipping some boy's butt for calling him a bad name reflecting on his Native American heritage. Abe did that pretty regularly for a while, until kids got tired of getting their asses handed to them. We became friends, probably because neither of us was a full-fledged, card-carrying member of the All-White Club. My African-American heritage was and is barely visible to the naked, unbigoted eye, but kids overhear their parents and some kids, in case you've forgotten, can be cruel as a hanging judge.

The all-white guys who later gravitated to us are still, along with Abe, my best friends. The ones who are left, R. P., Andy and Goat Johnson, are quite simply there for me. And nobody's been more "there" than Abe.

He taught me how to fight and how to keep from having to fight. He taught me how to know the point at which either fight or flight was inevitable, and how flight was just going to lead to another fight later on, so land the first punch and as many in a row as you can afterward, just to make your point.

After a while, nobody in his right mind called Abe a Tom-Tom, and nobody laid the n-word on me more than once. If the boy was bigger, I just waited until later and ambushed him, using whatever foreign object was at hand.

"They don't deserve a fair fight," was the way Abe Custalow, all of nine years old, explained it. Made sense to me.

Most of the kids I went to school with were decent, as kids go. A few of them, though, needed etiquette lessons. We gave them, free of charge.

Abe was always big for his age. I wasn't, so it sometimes was necessary to get people's attention. A kick in the balls usually did it. I did spend a fair amount of time in the principal's office, and once in a while I got suspended, but Peggy always stood behind me if my motives were pure, and sometimes even if they weren't.

"Just try not to get your butt killed," she told me once, when I was eleven. "Some of those little bastards might use more than their fists."

I found that out one day, a year later. Billy Ray Pitts had come to Oregon Hill when his father got five years in prison for his role in a bank robbery. Billy Ray, his brother and his mother, who'd been living somewhere on the North Side, had rented a place over on China Street, perhaps to be closer to Mr. Pitts, who now resided at the state penitentiary over across Belvidere. Billy Ray was ugly as a mud fence, with bad teeth and the onset of what would become a near-terminal case of acne. And, he was mean. It was said that the apple had not fallen far from the tree.

We were in the sixth grade. Billy Ray, being new to the neighborhood, hadn't learned all the social graces that made living in Oregon Hill so much more pleasant. He had not learned, among other things, not to fuck with Abe Custalow and Willie Black.

He was fearless, which isn't a bad thing, as long as you don't combine it with a near-fatal case of dumb. He had made a few borderline get-your-ass-kicked comments in school, at recess and in the lunchroom, and we let them pass, but Abe told me one day, a week before it happened, that there wasn't going to be but one way to shut up Billy Ray Pitts.

Billy Ray seemed to be assembling a little gang of like-minded future criminals around him. And then, he stepped in it.

The day it happened was in late September, so he had only known us for a few weeks.

He followed us home from school, staying half a block behind us. He had a couple of his new disciples with him, fifth-graders. They seemed to think it was funny when he'd throw a pebble, sometimes hitting us, sometimes not. Abe and I were handling it pretty well. I looked over once, for my cue, and Abe was smiling, like he was savoring an upcoming hearty meal of whip-ass.

Then, Billy Ray said the magic words.

Abe remembers it as, "Hey, it looks like Pow Wow the Indian Boy and the nigger are asshole buddies. Maybe they ought to get married."

I don't remember it quite like that, but I do remember the n-word.

When we dropped our books on the sidewalk and turned around, the fifth-graders sized up the situation in about two seconds, and then Billy Ray Pitts was on his own, just him and his mouth.

He started out standing his ground, and then, with us running toward him and his former acolytes hightailing it in the other direction, he turned and started running, too. Too late. I tackled him before he got to the corner, and we proceeded to kick his butt across the corner and halfway to his house. I'll admit, we were enjoying it. We'd let him get up and try to start running, then Abe would kick him to the curb or trip him, and we'd stomp him some more. The fifth-graders saw it all, staying at least a half block away, now firmly on our side.

By the time he got to his house and inside the front door, we were feeling our oats pretty good. We called him every kind of pussy we could think of. We banged on the front door and the windows. His mother was at work, and I guess Billy Ray's little brother was hiding under the bed by this time.

We were about to leave when the door opened. Billy Ray Pitts stepped out with a shotgun in his trembling, twelve-year-old hands.

"You can't talk to me like that," he said.

"How about if we kick your ass some more?" Abe said. "Is it OK if we do that?"

I suggested that maybe he should tell his jailbird father on us, come next visiting day.

The newborn lamb does not fear the lion. Twelve-year-old boys don't ever believe the gun is loaded. Abe started walking toward him, telling him if he didn't put the shotgun down, he was going to take it away from him and shove it up his ass.

Then, the gun went off. The noise and shock of it knocked me to the sidewalk. I looked up at Abe, halfway up the steps to Billy Ray by then. Somehow, the shot had missed him, and now he was just pissed off.

Billy Ray Pitts might not have meant to pull the trigger. His father probably left the gun there before he went away and maybe gave Billy Ray a quick lesson in loading and firing it, him being the man of the house and all. But he had this, "Oh, shit. What did I do?" look on his face. He got inside the door, sans shotgun, just ahead of Abe. If Abe had caught him, I don't think it would have been a positive outcome for either of them.

Nobody ever got arrested. One of the neighbors called the police, and the shell knocked a hole in the house across the street, but all they could get out of any of us was that Billy Ray had been showing us his father's gun and it accidentally went off. We might beat the little bastard senseless, but you didn't collaborate with the cops. And our erstwhile tormentor had been well trained along those lines. He said he tripped on the sidewalk.

"Yeah," I remember the cop saying, "maybe seven or eight times, it looks like." But they let it, and us, go.

It was the last time Peggy ever hit me. Peggy never planned corporal punishment; it just happened. When she came home from work, after hearing the story from two neighbors before she'd even gotten in the door, she just dropped the bag of groceries on the floor and started boxing my ears. I let her, protecting myself as best I could. Then, she wrapped her arms around me so hard I couldn't breathe.

"You little shit," she said. "If something happened to you, I'd die."

I once stumbled on a quote from George Bernard Shaw. I looked it up the other day:

"If you strike a child, take care that you strike it in anger, even at the risk of maiming it for life. A blow in cold blood neither can nor should be forgiven."

Peggy never read George Bernard Shaw, but they had the same philosophy on child rearing.

Abe Custalow and I survived our childhoods and have muddled through what probably is the majority of our adulthoods, wandering in and out of each other's lives. Bringing him to share the apartment has worked out well for both of us, seldom more so on my behalf than right now.

I PHONED Finlay Rand after I got home last night. He seemed to be in what Clara Westbrook or one of our other Prestwould grand dames would call "a state."

"I don't know what to do," he said. "He's going to kill me. I know he is."

I told Rand all I've learned about who Raymond Gatewood has and hasn't been talking to. It didn't seem to appease him.

"And the paper keeps running all those stories. Why can't this just go away? And why do they always have to use my name?"

I'm not very long on patience with Mr. Rand these days. I reminded him that the latest story ran because Les Hacker died, and that it was essential to explain why Les's death was a big deal, especially to Mr. Gatewood, who is now facing life in prison or worse. I reminded him that this was a great personal sorrow to me. I refrained from telling him to go fuck himself.

"Yes, of course," he said, getting a grip. "And I am sorry for your loss. I didn't realize. Where can I send flowers?"

I gave him Peggy's address and told him, once again, that I didn't think he had anything to worry about. Custalow came in while I was still on the phone. He was frowning, and he had a couple of videotapes in his hands.

Rand was still talking when I hung up.

"That guy's nuts," I said. Abe just walked over to the TV.

"This is what I wanted to show you."

He said that something was nagging him, right from the beginning, about the shooting.

"They had the video of the guy in the wig and the sports jacket, leaving the building," he said. "But where did he come from? When did he get in?"

I said that I assumed he got in the same way he got back out again. Somebody's always leaving that back door cracked open, either accidentally or on purpose.

"Yeah. I know. I have to close it about every other day. But we videotape that basement door every day, not just the day Les got shot."

I thought about this for a few seconds. Then the twenty-watt light bulb that powers my thimble-size brain flickered on.

"Yeah," Abe said. "So, if we assume the guy got in the same way he got out, that would be on the videotape, too, right?"

I nodded my head and wondered why Richmond's finest didn't figure this out. Or why the inestimable law firm of Marcus Green and Ex-Wife didn't think of it. Well, hell. I didn't either.

It took the cranial capacity of Abraham Custalow to deduce the obvious.

He went back two days on the tapes of the basement door, he said. He never saw anyone vaguely resembling Raymond Gatewood come in.

"But this is what I did find." One of the videotapes was for April 3, two days before Les was shot. He put it in and fast-forwarded it to a certain spot, then stopped it.

"Watch this."

He started the tape again, at about double speed. It was like watching paint dry. But then I saw someone enter the door. Abe rewound, and we watched it at real speed.

He ran it twice, just so I could make sure I was seeing what I was seeing.

"Son of a bitch," was all I could say.

I SMOKED, drank and slept on it last night after talking to Abe. Didn't get to bed until after two.

Today, I went for a walk, had a late breakfast at Perly's and then went into the office just to clear my head. It's definitely time to have another discussion with Chief L. D. Jones, and another one with Green and Kate. But I'm stalling. Knowledge is power, and it almost gives me a hard-on to have this kind of information and not share it with anyone. I hoard information the way the Koch brothers hoard money, not wanting to let anyone have a slice until I can present the whole package with a nice bow on top, so everybody says what a smart boy I am.

This can be a problem, but it's my problem.

Sarah comes in while I'm looking stuff up. Ed Chenowith isn't in today, but with Sarah's help I'm able to find much of what I was looking for.

"Hurry up," she says, and I know she's not talking about my little search. "Wheelie's got me covering city hall and your beat, too, and he says Grubby won't sign off on overtime. He said I could take comp time later, and then he gave me some bullshit speech about working for myself, not wanting to wake up one day and realize I'd just punched a clock. I wanted to punch him."

I tell her they used to work that scam on me, too, although they did pay for overtime back then. They're supposed to now, but in our business-friendly state, your employer has the right to work you like a dog and hire somebody else when you don't roll over and fetch.

I also tell her, though, that sometimes you really do have to play their game to get where you're going. If you work over-time for free and win a Pulitzer Prize, you can go to the copier, pull your dress up, pull your panties down, hop up and photo-copy your bottom. Then you can take the photocopy, march up to Grubby's office, hand it to him and tell him to kiss it.

"Nice image," she says, rolling her eyes. "It'd probably get him excited."

"It'd do it for me," I say.

"Oh," Sarah says. "I thought you'd retired."

"Just trying to flaunt my self-control."

I ask her if she and Mark Baer are still an item.

"An item? How old did you say you were, anyhow? Yeah, we still hang out, you know."

It's like talking to Andi. Whenever I try to delicately extract information from my daughter about her boyfriend, roommate, drinking buddy, whatever, Thomas Jefferson Blandford V, she gets as slippery as a greased eel.

"What are you doing, anyhow?" she asks, looking over my shoulder.

I explain as much as I can without giving it all away.

"I'm sorry about that guy, Les, by the way," she said, put-ting one of her warm hands on my neck. The slight connec-tion of bare skin to bare skin is like an electric shock, enough to trigger a flashback. Must be age appropriate. Must be age appropriate. "I met him once. He was with you at a Squirrels game, I think. He seemed like a really good guy."

I assure her that he was. It is too much information to add that he was the closest thing to a father I ever had, but I say it anyhow.

She gives out the kind of "awww" that women seem to emit when they see kittens, babies or orphaned fire victims. It's a multipurpose sound apparently indicating empathy of one kind or another. She hugs me. I wasn't fishing for one, honest.

I thank her for her concern. She asks me when the funeral is. I tell her and assure her that she won't be written out of my book of life if she doesn't come. She tells me to shut up, but in a nice way.

She walks away. It is a pleasure to watch Sarah Goodnight walk away, especially on casual Saturday, when jeans are permitted.

Someone clears his throat behind me. I don't know how long James H. Grubbs has been standing there. Not too long, I hope.

"So," he says "are you back with us? Or have you decided to spend the rest of your working career, however long that may be, chasing ballplayers?"

I remind Grubby that I am, after all, on my own dime now, burning up what little vacation time I've accrued since my last luxurious sojourn, which I spent on Andy Peroni's houseboat on Lake Anna. It's moored just below the nuclear plant. Even if the kids didn't pee in the water, it'd still be warm.

"Nevertheless, we do expect you back in the not-too-distant future," he says. "Your beat isn't covering itself."

"No, it's being covered by a kid who's still naïve enough to work for free."

"We pay our employees well. Some of them, too well." He gives me his best gimlet-eyed laser beam.

Grubby doesn't want to know his newsroom managers are running afoul of the National Labor Relations Board, which has succeeded in spanking our ass on occasion when some of our corporate types have gone beyond even the Pluto-distant boundaries of what is and isn't allowed in our right-to-work paradise.

I can imagine his conversation with Wheelie re: Sarah Goodnight.

Wheelie: If she covers night cops and city hall, we're going to have to pay her overtime.

Grubby: We don't pay overtime.

Wheelie: Well, how are we going to do it?

Grubby: That's up to you.

Grubby (unspoken): Just don't tell me about it.

"At any rate," Grubby continues now, "it won't be a problem for very much longer, one way or the other."

"One way or the other?"

"One more week," he says, holding up his index finger. "Then you're back."

Message received. For some reason, journalism schools—excuse me, mass communications schools—are still turning out bright-eyed, hungry newshounds who would do my job for half of what I require.

I might be back with a story that'll knock your dick off, I want to tell him.

KATE IS in her makeshift quarters at Marcus Green's office. It's just up the street, and I thought I might be able to catch the great man himself. But it's a fine day for golf, and I know Marcus is now a jovial, backslapping member of one of the local country clubs that would only have let him in as a caddy in the not-too-distant past.

What I want to know is why Kate is spending a fine Saturday indoors.

"I'm researching," she says. "Marcus can sell ice to the Eskimos, but he's not so good on dotting the i's, crossing the t's. That, I can do."

She's looking for an angle, some way to make Raymond Gatewood a little less guilty than he appears. And if he's found guilty, a way to make him seem as crazy as possible. She's looking for precedents.

I can't bear to let Kate work this hard for no good reason. I tell her who didn't come in the basement door for at least two days before the shooting.

She rewards me by throwing a rather hefty law book in my direction.

"How long have you known all this?"

"Not long," I say, picking it up and handing it back to her. "And you really shouldn't be lifting something that heavy." Let alone throwing it.

I wonder aloud why neither she nor Marcus had thought to check on that.

She throws her hands up.

"Hell, I don't know. We should have. We're just not as smart as you, I guess."

I let her off the hook by telling her that checking the previous days' tapes wasn't exactly my idea.

"So he hadn't come in the basement door for two days before this happened? But maybe he was in there for several days. Or maybe he came in the front door."

I remind her that it's a little harder for a guy who looks every bit as homeless as he is to get past our crack security guards, let alone have a fob or get himself buzzed into the building. I also remind her that it didn't appear that anyone had been there for very long before the shooting. No food strewn about. The place wasn't trashed. The toilets were flushed. No one had taken a dump on the Oriental rug. And there's something else, something that didn't occur to me until Custalow showed me that tape. When Awesome began living at Peggy's place, she and Les soon became aware that he had to start becoming more intimate with soap and water. The English basement smelled like holy hell for a month after he got there. By the time I walked in on the cops inspecting Finlay Rand's place, it smelled like I imagine Finlay Rand's place always smells, like a tastefully done French whorehouse. No *eau de bum*.

It's time to tell Kate who *was* seen coming in the basement door of the Prestwould on April 3.

"Are you kidding me?" she says. "Really?"

Yes, I tell her. Really.

"Well," she says, "maybe it's time to have another chat with your good friend L. D. Jones."

"He'd probably just tell me to go fuck myself."

"I imagine people do that all the time."

I tell Kate that I'd rather wait a day or two. The cops aren't going to turn Raymond Gatewood loose on the flimsy evidence I can show them on the videotape. They don't want to turn him loose at all.

"This is bullshit," she says. "You just want to do it all yourself, don't you?"

"I just want to have something a little more solid to go on."

"Nah. Nah. I know you. You're going to be Mister Solo."

I remind her that I've already told her more than she was ever going to figure out on her own—what happened to the other Vees, who did and didn't come in through the Prestwould's basement door in the two days leading up to Les's shooting.

I explain that the only reason her client has a snowball's chance in hell of getting out from under Les Hacker's murder is because of my unpaid, vacation-burning dedication.

She is quiet, which is unusual for Kate.

"OK," she says at last. "You've earned the right to say that, although I believe we eventually would have thought of looking at those other tapes. But we need to bring the police in."

"One more day," I tell her, holding my index finger in the air, Grubby-like.

I walk back to the paper in the remnants of a beautiful spring afternoon. The Squirrels are home tonight, and it'd be great to take in a few innings, at least until the night chill rolled in to remind us that it's still April. But I have promises to keep.

I'm to be over at Peggy's by six, so we can lock in on some of the memorial plans. Monday's just two days away. One of Les's brothers, a few years younger, is flying in from Wisconsin, along with his daughter. The phone hasn't stopped ringing off the hook at Peggy's. It appears that Les knew approximately half the damn town, and now we're wondering if the Baptist church will be big enough to hold everybody.

I made sure that I called Buck McRae to tell him the sad news. He said he was coming up. I tried to dissuade him, and it seemed to offend him.

"Whoever shot Les," I explained to the ancient right fielder, "might still be out there. I have reason to believe that."

"Bullshit," Buck said. "I'm coming. It's like they say, if we're afraid, the terrorists win."

I start to ask him what the hell this has to do with terrorists, but maybe he's right. Whoever goes around killing old minor-league baseball players is as much a terrorist as the late, hell-residing Osama bin Laden.

I told Buck that he and whoever drives him up here are welcome to stay with Abe and me.

"I can drive my own damn self up," he said. "But I thank you for the invitation."

I tell him to be careful.

"I didn't get this far," he said before he hung up, "by being careful."

BEFORE I go over to Peggy's, though, I need to do some more research. There is still a lot of "why?" to unravel.

I'm back at my desk, scribbling on the pad next to me, collecting printouts and going back over notes from my odyssey so far. I am, in short, trying to make sense out of lunacy.

I've written down lots of names: All the 1964 Vees and their survivors, then August Harshman, Eleanor Harshman Flynn Fairchild, Dairy Flynn. I cross out Dairy and write in his real name.

I used to pass the time in windbag legislative sessions and later waiting for the next East End shooting by doing the crossword puzzle and then the word jumble. You take six or seven random letters and try to make the biggest word you can out of them. I got pretty good at it. I got so it was almost like instinct.

Now, looking at Dairy Flynn's given name, it hits me.

"Son of a bitch."

Chapter Eighteen

SUNDAY

*I*f God gives mulligans, and you only have three for your entire life, I'll take one of mine for last night. Failing that, I'm praying that Cindy Peroni gives them.

When I called at Rand's apartment, I got a recording. When I got back to the Prestwould, I took the elevator up to the ninth floor and knocked, but nobody answered.

It was time then to go over to Peggy's and be of some use to my mother. The place was almost as full of people as it had been on Thursday night, and now the guests, instead of bringing food, were eating it. I suppose it's a good idea to bring something to the bereaved that you yourself wouldn't mind chowing down on a couple of days later. By the time the post-funeral crowd gets through on Monday, Peggy's fridge will be as empty as it was before Les died.

My mother's never been much of a hostess. She never did big holiday family dinners, mainly because most of her family had abandoned her. She and I spent most of our Christmas days in the company of each other. We were fond of the whole barbecued chicken Peggy's employer for most of my tween and teen years gave out in lieu of actual money. We'd feast on it for a couple of days, then go back to frozen dinners and whatever I could manage not to ruin. My repertoire was somewhat small, but Peggy was too busy earning a living to really learn how to cook, and even before I reached the age of reason (if, indeed, I have reached it yet), I knew that it wasn't really a good idea to let my mother loose in the kitchen after she'd had her post-work smoke. Stoned, she was certainly better company than the hard drinkers some of my friends got stuck with for parents, but she was something of a fire hazard.

As far as parties, whatever Oregon Hill soirees occurred at our rental house of the moment mostly consisted of people bringing their own beer or jug wine, with Peggy supplying the Fritos and onion dip. If things got really fancy, she'd have me grill hot dogs.

Last night, though, Andi and Cindy took over. My daughter is a pro at serving the public, having spent as much of the last three years dispensing food and drink as she has pursuing that ever-elusive VCU diploma. With her degree destination somewhere in the neighborhood of psychology, sociology or English, I suppose it's good that she has marketable skills. She worked her way through the crowd with whatever she and Cindy could stuff into those little dinner rolls everybody in town buys at the grocery store. And Cindy showed an amazing dexterity in slicing the country ham someone donated into razor thin slices. I believe she could have fed the five thousand with this one damn piece of pork, as long as the rolls didn't run out, and they sent me out for more.

Why, in the worst week of your life, do you have to serve and entertain?

Some people brought their own liquor or beer and braved the chill on the porch to take the edge off somebody else's loss. Peggy disappeared every hour or so. She has gotten pretty good at self-medicating, managing to stave off the grief without becoming a dope zombie.

I tried Rand's number again. No luck.

By nine thirty, the crowd was starting to break up. Most of the really good food was gone by then, anyhow. The crowd didn't seem to be pacing itself well; most of the tasty stuff had disappeared, and a lot of Jell-O salads and cold, store-bought fried chicken littered Peggy's dining room table. Cindy whispered to me that we might have to buy more food for the Sunday and Monday moochers, er, mourners.

"God," Peggy said as she tripped and nearly knocked me over, "won't these assholes ever leave?"

I know she appreciates the company, but she could use some rest.

Cindy takes her back to the bedroom, perhaps to lie down rather than toke up this time.

Awesome Dude came in the house sometime after nine from Lord knows where. Awesome is hurting. Les was one of those rare creatures who treated everyone like equals, and Awesome hasn't had a lot of that in his life. My hope is that he and my mother can keep their addled, jerry-built little family standing without Les around as the support beam.

Awesome tried to help us clean up, and we appreciated the effort if not the results. Guys who are used to scooping pork and beans out of a can with their fingers aren't very fussy about removing food particles from dishes.

Sometime before eleven, the last of the guests left. Peggy was asleep, with some help from the little magic pill Cindy gave her. Andi said she had to get back to her apartment, where Thomas Jefferson Blandford V, a.k.a. Quint, no doubt awaited, probably in his smoking jacket. I still haven't met His Highness.

I suggested to Cindy that we get out for a little while. The night is still young, I told her, meaning I haven't had nearly enough to drink.

She said she was tired, meaning she probably knew what I meant. I should have been zonked, too, but nervous energy was keeping me going.

Cindy didn't want me to be, or drink, alone, I guess, and she finally agreed to come along. She suggested O'Toole's, over on Forest Hill, a place I remember fondly from my earlier newspaper years.

Last night did not add to those fond memories.

It is almost always a bad idea on my part to come into a bar late. There is a sense, as the clock ticks toward closing time, that one has to catch up with the lucky bastards who've been there all night. This can cause problems.

I ran into an old high school buddy who left a long time ago and wanted to wax nostalgic about the Hill. I suppose I kind of lost touch with Cindy, who ran into Becky somebody and Susan somebody from her married past. Consequently, she wasn't there to gently suggest that I slow the fuck down.

There was a sense of entitlement. My almost-dad is going to be buried on Monday, I'm so sad. Boo-hoo-hoo. Pour me another. My little brain, the one in charge of things like sex, smoking and drinking, is very good at whispering the magic words into my receptive ears. You've had a tough day. You need to unwind.

By one thirty, I was shit-faced. I went looking for Cindy, who I realized I hadn't seen in about an hour and a half. I found her dancing with some guy. He wasn't doing much, I guess, but it was a slow dance, and he seemed to have his arm far enough below her waist to warrant a cut-in.

When I made my move, the guy made a slight mistake. He told me to fuck off. This would not have sat well with me if, theoretically, I were in a bar and had been drinking Coca-Colas all night.

After six or seven bourbons on the rocks, the little warning light governing proper etiquette when your date is getting her ass felt up had long since burned out.

The guy wasn't much bigger than me, but he probably was ten or fifteen years younger, and I'm lucky that it was a one-punch fight.

Cindy pushed me away, and the guy's buddy held him back (it didn't take too much effort, I have to say). I was lucky that there were no cops on the premises. O'Toole's, like most bars, can do without the free publicity you get when the blue lights come charging in like the cavalry around closing time.

But that's pretty much where my luck ran out. In my clue-lessness, I figured that it was time to take Cindy home, and that she'd think it was kind of gallant of me to deck the guy who was taking liberties with her.

She showed me the error of my ways.

"You asshole," she explained when we were outside and headed for my car. "That was Becky's brother-in-law. We were just dancing. What's wrong with you?"

"He had his hand on your ass."

"So what? Willie, I'm past forty, I'm divorced and I've spent the last two hours being ignored by the guy who brought me here. It's my ass, and he can grab it if he wants to. And he wasn't grabbing it, he was fondling it. And I was letting him."

I realize, in morning's cruel light, that an apology of some sort might have been in order on my part. What probably wasn't in order was calling Cindy Peroni a bad name.

She looked like she wanted to hit me. She might have, if I hadn't turned sideways at the last minute and thrown up on the side of my car.

A slap would have hurt less than what she said. She said it sober and sorrowful.

"This is what I was talking about, Willie. Life's too short."

And she turned and walked off, calling after one of her old friends—or maybe it was the guy I punched—to take her to somebody's home while I tried to clean off the side of my car and then fell on the asphalt as I tried to go after her.

I somehow managed to get myself back to the Prestwould without picking up another DUI. One piece of good luck on a hard-luck night.

THIS IS one of those mornings when you want to take down the mirrors. I haven't told Custalow everything that happened last night. By the look he gives me, though, he gets the gist of it: Willie fucked up again.

One thing I've always prided myself on: I can separate the train wreck of my civilian life from work. Work has sustained me, really, in the times after I screwed up marriages one, two and three, in the days when I failed so miserably as a father, when I've awakened the next morning with almost enough remorse to swear off drinking.

And there is work to do.

I tell Abe about Dairy Flynn's name. I show him. He whistles.

"I'll be damned. I'll be damned."

Then, the obvious question.

"So what are you going to do?"

I tell him that I don't have a plan yet, but I'm working on one. What I ought to do is call the cops. Surely Peachy Love can find me somebody over there who won't turn a deaf ear to a career-enhancing tip. Even Gillespie would put down his doughnut and jump on this one.

Still, I tell myself, there are a couple of loose ends. I want to hand it over to either the cops or our readers or both as signed, sealed and delivered, no postage due.

Rand doesn't answer when I call again, and I don't have time to go up there now anyhow. As usual, I'm late.

I promised to run by Peggy's. We have to see the minister about tomorrow's service. He said he would come by around nine thirty, before the eleven o'clock service at the Baptist church where Peggy and I used to go on Easter and Christmas most years. I may still be the closest thing to a true-blue African-American to have crossed Mount Hebron's threshold. The "new" minister has been there for six years, but I'm pretty sure he and Peggy had never met until she needed someone to perform a funeral.

When I get there, Rev. Gladfelter's car is parked in front and it's nine thirty-five. Peggy glares at me but doesn't say anything. There is a fog of air freshener hanging over the living room, in case the reverend is also a narc.

We talk about Les, giving the minister of our erstwhile church a brief description of a life well lived.

"And," he says, clearing his throat, "you and, uh, Les, you were engaged?"

"Well," Peggy says, "I guess you could say that."

Rev. Gladfelter lets it pass, probably wondering how he's going to explain it all to the gathering tomorrow, as if everyone on Oregon Hill didn't know Peggy and Les's ringless status. Well, either way, the rev gets paid. The newspaper obit, written by yours truly, says Leslie Michael Hacker is survived by his brother and niece, who arrived last night, and his special friend, Margaret Warren Black. Les probably wouldn't have been pleased to have his whole name revealed to the world, but it seemed like it should be out there at least once, for the record.

By the time the minister leaves, I'm feeling pretty certain that tomorrow's service, done by a man Les never met, will go well.

When he leaves, Peggy dashes off to the bedroom and comes back in a couple of minutes with her eyes somewhat dilated.

"Thank God," she says. "Awesome and me were up half the night cleaning this place. Nobody ought have to go through this straight."

I remind her that it's still not ten o'clock.

"Seems like it's about four in the afternoon. Oh. Wait here. There's something I want you to take back with you."

She goes into the bedroom again and comes out with a cardboard box. Inside are some old photos and programs, mementos of Les's baseball days. I pull out a photo that's marked, "1964 Richmond Vees," and there's Les. I can make out most of the other starters from photos I've accumulated. Buck McRae is standing on the end, with a space between him and Roy Haas.

Beneath those is Les's catcher's mitt. He said he'd had it since he was in Class-A ball. Kept it through ten years in the minors. It's a relic, a great big dinosaur of a thing compared to the ones the catchers wear now. Sometimes, especially in recent years when his mind began to take little walkabouts, he would sit watching TV with the mitt on his big left hand. He would carry it with him on his perambulations. Sometimes an acquaintance would find him, several blocks away, standing on a street corner with the mitt on his hand as if he expected God to throw him a high, hard one.

"He wanted you to have all that," Peggy says. "I guess he's left everything else to me."

For some reason, the mitt, with its stuffing on the verge of popping out and its leather worn nearly gray, breaks me up. My mom and I have a good cry.

I promise Peggy, before I leave, that the person who shot Les Hacker is going to pay. I promise her justice.

On the way out, I meet Jumpin' Jimmy. He has come over to see if there's any way he can help. It's time to bring Jimmy Deacon up to speed.

The first thing I ask him is whether he's made any trips to Wells, Vermont, in the recent past.

"Jumpin' Jimmy hasn't been out of the environment of Richmond since my brother and me went to the Outer Banks last fall when the blues was biting," he says.

He gets it after a few seconds.

"You mean, where Frannie came from?"

I explain my recent trip up there, and I tell him more than I mean to about the fate of Les's teammates.

When I tell him that, no, I haven't gone to the cops yet, even Jimmy can see that this is not necessarily the smartest move.

I tell him that I'm not famous for being smart.

BACK AT the Prestwould, Feldman is holding court there as usual. I swear, sometimes I think McGrumpy has sold his unit and lives in the lobby. Custalow says he saw him eating lunch the other day in one of the chairs by the guard's desk.

Clara Westbrook seems relieved to have an excuse to break away from our resident pest.

"Is intrigue afoot?" Feldman asks, his eyebrows rising and falling like a couple of caterpillars on his aged brow.

I tell him there's an ax murderer on the loose, and that he's looking for snoopy old men.

Upstairs, I call again and finally am able to rouse the man who has seemed so anxious to bend my ear of late.

"Yes," Finlay Rand says, "how may I help you?"

I identify myself and tell him that he can help me, perhaps, by telling me why he cut his recent vacation short and returned to the Prestwould two days before his apartment was broken into.

He's silent while I explain about the camera that caught him coming into the building via the basement two days before Les was plugged.

"That's impossible," he says. "I was lying on a hammock on Virgin Gorda at the time your mother's boyfriend was shot. I didn't get back here until the Tuesday afterward."

I tell him that I have some more information that I've dug up, things he might be interested in knowing about the 1964 Richmond Vees. He doesn't say anything for what seems like half a minute. I wonder if he's hung up.

"There's something you need to know," he says, at last. "It's about those calls I've been getting. But I need you to come up here. Be here in one hour."

I tell him that I can be there right now, but he says that won't work.

"One hour."

Custalow says he should go up with me, but Rand made it clear that it had to be just the two of us, one on one.

"You know where I am," I tell him. "If he shoots me, you'll know who did it."

I wait an hour, then tell Abe that, if I'm not back in forty-five minutes, to come get me. He shakes his head and calls me a dumb ass.

At my appointed hour, I walk up the three flights to Rand's unit. I could use the exercise. It is somewhat disappointing that I have to stop to catch my breath between the seventh and eighth floors. Geez, Peggy would say, you think maybe you should quit smoking?

I knock on the door and wait. I knock again. I put my ear to the doorframe, and I don't hear anything or anybody inside.

I turn the knob. The door opens.

I call to Finlay Rand. No one answers.

Inside, I walk down the foyer, past all of Rand's art collection and the second and third bedrooms, to the living room, dining room and kitchen. I call again. There's nobody home.

I think for a moment that Mr. Rand has taken it on the lam. Then I turn around and look back in the direction I came from. Beside the entrance is the doorway leading to the rest of Rand's unit. In my place, which is twice the size of the place where Peggy raised me, the door leads to a big-ass master bedroom back there. Rand's apartment, though, has something extra. Sometime in the distant past, a Prestwould resident must have bought the bedroom in the unit that backs up to this one and claimed it as his own. I can barely see all the way to the other end of Rand's digs, because past the master bedroom at the other end of the foyer there's another room, just as big. There's a light on back there.

When I call Rand's name again, there's no answer, but I think I hear something off in the distance.

Nothing to do but go back there.

Past the foyer, where Rand's art is highlighted by wall lights, the bedroom is pitch dark. He must have put up blackout curtains. I trip over something and go toward the light, which offers just enough illumination to get me to the back room.

I walk through the open door and call Rand's name again.

Then, the lights go out.

Chapter Nineteen

*W*hen I come to, I have a flashback to my Great Aunt Celia's. She was the only member of Peggy's unforgiving family to offer my mother sustenance after it became obvious that she had shamed the Black family by having sex at least once with an African-American who was somewhat lackadaisical about birth control (as, apparently, was Peggy).

Anyhow, Celia was the one member of the family who amounted to something, at least judging by bank accounts. By the time Peggy and her "black bastard baby" were being shown the door, Celia had managed to own a substantial house and several rental properties, one of which became the first haven for Peggy and me.

Celia's house was on the North Side, over near Richmond Memorial. Celia lived there by herself, having decided that male companionship was not essential to her happiness. Sometimes, she'd invite me over when I was a little kid. She'd make great meals, and she and her friend Connie did their best to make me smile and even laugh.

One of the things they would do was play hide-and-seek with me. The house had three floors and a basement, and we would take turns hiding. Sometimes, I'd go to the third floor and wedge myself into the nook of an unused room full of books and clothes and age. They would find me, of course.

They probably knew exactly where I was all along, just from listening to my footsteps, but they always dragged it out, finally pouncing on me as I squealed with glee.

That memory of that smell is imprinted on my brain. Sometimes, when I'm in one of the older Prestwouldian's digs, I'll get a flashback to those days. It's the smell of mustiness, comfort and drowsy Saturday afternoons.

I'm afraid, though, that the smell will, in the future, evoke a less pleasant memory. I can thank Finlay Rand for that.

"WELL, WELL, Mr. Black," Rand says, still holding the metal pipe he must have used to coldcock me, "and how are we feeling?"

I am handcuffed to something that isn't moving. A blindfold isn't necessary, although I am gagged. The Finlay Rand who hovers over me looks less helpless than I've ever seen him.

I want to rub the large knot I feel growing on the back of my skull. I would like about a dozen Advils, a pint of bourbon and a cigarette. I am in a world of pain. I seem to be surrounded by the kind of crap Finlay Rand buys cheap and sells high.

"I don't know about you," I manage to croak out through the gag, "but I'm feeling like shit."

"I'm sorry for your discomfort," he says, "but it was important to bring you here. You've been very persistent, Mr. Black, so persistent that I find myself cornered. But, no worries. It had to happen sometime."

He sets down the pipe.

"It would be a shame, though, to have this, this masterpiece go unrecognized. You see, I am an artist, Mr. Black, and my canvas is revenge."

He sighs.

"I can't know if you've called the police, and I surely wouldn't trust you to tell the truth in your present circumstances. Whether you did or not, I don't expect to have very long to lay out the breadth of what I have accomplished. How much, by the way, do you know? Surely you weren't fooled for long by my fictitious tormentor, or by that unfortunate soul who happened to take the coat I left in the park. I can't believe how long it took those feckless police to find that key."

He shakes his head and removes the gag momentarily.

I tell him that all I know is that he killed an innocent man.

"You mean Mr. Hacker. Ah, you would say that. But they were all there, Mr. Black. They all could have stopped it. And if a few relative innocents have to meet their maker along the way, well, as someone or other has been saying since The Crusades, let God sort them out."

I tell him that I know about the others. Hell, he's got to know that anyhow.

"Ah, yes. When you told me you saw me enter the Prest-would two days before the shooting, I knew that, as they say, the jig was up. I already knew that you were researching that benighted group of thugs. I felt certain that a hard-nosed reporter such as yourself would not rest until he got to the bottom.

"Well, Mr. Black, you have found the bottom. Let me tell you a story."

LITTLE DAIRY Flynn adored his big sister. Frances Flynn was, I gather through the filter of an obviously biased witness, about the only thing worth having in the little boy's life.

"She was beautiful and sweet and wonderful. And then she left."

She came back, of course, but their parents made her leave again when they found out she was pregnant.

"Dairy never forgave them for that, and after she died, after those knuckle-dragging animals killed her, nothing much mattered to him anymore. He became something of a, shall we say, problem child."

He drifted in and out of his family's orbit. The last time he disappeared, working on a lobster boat, he came close to killing himself.

"He actually stood on the edge of the pier, with a cinder block tied around his neck, teetering on the edge. But he couldn't make himself do it.

"And then he met Walter LeForge."

LeForge was a wealthy yachtsman and confirmed bachelor. Dairy, a handsome lad who resembled his sister, had taken one odd job after another around the docks, where he often came in contact with people who could afford to do nothing but sail. One day, he caught LeForge's fancy. He took him on as what might be thought of euphemistically as a cabin boy.

"Oh, it wasn't so bad," Rand says now. "It's really all the same, you know, when you close your eyes. One does what one has to do. And he taught little Dairy some things. Other than in bed, I mean."

LeForge, born into money, had made a small fortune larger as an art dealer. He recognized soon after taking Dairy Flynn on that the boy had a natural intellect and an almost eerie ability to pick the wheat from the chaff.

By 1975, when Dairy turned twenty-one, he changed his name. He didn't want anyone who ever knew him to find him again.

"Dairy thought they might get curious about how his stepfather, the upstanding Roger Fairchild, died. It was best that he disappear and be reborn. I'd tell you the whole story about poor Roger, but then I'd have to kill you."

He laughs at his own joke, the only time I've ever seen him laugh.

"Suffice it to say that, fine swimmer that he was, Roger couldn't overcome handcuffs and a pair of cinder blocks. If it was good enough for Dairy to consider for himself, surely it was good enough for his dear old stepdad.

"He hadn't seen me for two years when I surprised him on his boat that night. He begged for mercy, and then, when he realized that he was going to be thrown overboard helpless and alive, he begged me to shoot him."

Finlay Rand wipes his forehead. We could use some air conditioning in here.

"It was almost erotic."

LeForge adopted Dairy Flynn and took care of changing his name and his whole identity.

"He wanted me to change it to LeForge, but I persuaded him to let me name myself. I though Finlay Rand was rather clever. You did get the joke, didn't you, Mr. Black? No one else did."

I nod my head. Adair Flynn becomes Finlay Rand. Willie Black nominated for the Word Scramble Pulitzer. Posthumously, apparently.

"And, of course, Walter LaForge had to be done away with, if I was going to have the life I wanted, the life to which I was entitled. By this time, I'd gotten rather adept at disappearances at sea. LaForge's family threw a fit, of course. He had a brother and sister who could have used the money I inherited. But neither of them had spoken to poor Walter in five years. They deserved what they got, which was nothing. There was nobody but his heartbroken adopted son on board when Walter went over in the middle of the night. People had their suspicions. A cursory investigation was conducted, but I made very certain that no body ever surfaced."

He sits on one of the dusty antique chairs. It's covered in plastic, I guess so the priceless fabric will be untouched by human ass. He's calm and mad as a hatter.

"You see, I had a dream. I dreamed that one day all those subhuman bastards who caused Frannie to end her life, really end my life, too, would pay the ultimate price. It was only fair.

"I had money, and I had time."

He said he got most of what he knows about Frannie's demise from his mother, who had managed to get in touch with the last girl Frannie roomed with in Richmond. Frannie had told the girl, who knew she had gone to Florida with the expectation of marrying Lucky Whitestone, what happened down there. Then Frannie ignored the girl's pleas to stay and went to her suicide bed.

"Perhaps your, uh, friend wasn't as culpable as some, but nobody stepped in."

He pauses and looks off into a dark corner of this dreary room.

"Frannie wasn't perfect, but she had a good, trusting heart. I knew that when I was ten years old, Mr. Black. She came to my room, the night before she ran away. She said she had to see something bigger than Wells, Vermont, and that someday I'd understand. I didn't really blame her. Our father was capable of almost anything, and Mother always seemed to take his side. It was Frannie and me against the world.

"She left me this." He pulls on the necklace around his neck and extracts a ring. It's a high school ring, the one Frannie must have gotten before she dropped out and went south.

"I've been wearing this for forty-seven years. She said she'd be back. And she would have come, if they hadn't killed her."

I try to speak. Rand loosens the gag and sits down again.

"They didn't kill her. She killed herself."

This doesn't seem to please him. He stands, walks over and gives me a not-so-light tap on my head with the pipe, then regags me when I scream.

"She would have come back. But they killed her spirit. She had no place left to go. Our parents would not have taken her back, damn their souls."

He sets the pipe down again.

"But Frannie has been avenged."

Like so many people I've interviewed over the years, he is dying to tell his story. He just needs someone to shut up and listen—in this case, someone who has no choice. I am not optimistic that I'll be telling this to anyone else, but Rand offers me a little hope.

"You might live to regale your readers with this, uh, adventure, Mr. Black. I haven't made up my mind yet. One thing is certain, though. I won't be telling it."

He lifts his jacket and I see the pistol.

"Bullets for two," he says. "Maybe I'll use them both, maybe not."

You first, I'm thinking, but it hasn't been my lucky day so far.

"So, it's story time, Mr. Black."

He took over much of Walter LeForge's business. It was a trade that allowed him to travel widely.

"It suited my purposes. And dealing with an extensive variety of valuable items enabled me to become adept at some things that might surprise you, like weaponry, detective work and even spycraft. And I knew a good bit about nautical matters already.

"And, I was patient. No need to hurry. Life is long. And what's the saying? Revenge is best served cold?"

He sits down again.

"I had been Finlay Rand for ten years when I started. I'd been putting it off for years, just because I could, but one day I woke and decided I had to follow my dream."

He smiles at this, obviously cracking himself up. He's a riot.

Rand was living in Atlanta, and he had the same 1964 Richmond Vees opening-day lineup he'd been carrying around in his wallet since not long after Frannie's suicide.

Phil Holt, he discovered, wasn't living that far away, and Rand often went to Mobile to buy old shit.

"The first time is always the most memorable," he says. "The adrenaline rush was amazing. I mean, I had dispatched people before, as you and I know, but this was a mission, and I saw it as my sacred duty. Sacred, Mr. Black."

He says Holt never really knew what hit him. He thought he was being robbed at gunpoint.

"He seemed to know what to do. It probably had happened to him before. It was a sad, nasty little store. I gathered that Mr. Holt had squandered whatever riches he might have gained playing that silly game."

With just the two of them in the store, Rand says he had time to explain to Holt who he was and why Holt was going to die.

"I don't think he 'got it,' though. And finally, I just shot him. Once in the heart and once in the head. I was halfway back to Atlanta before they found the body."

He waited three years.

"I knew that Mr. Whitestone was the worst one," he says. "I knew he was the one who promised to marry her and then instigated that cruel trick on what she thought would be her wedding night. I wanted him to suffer the most of all, but you have to take your opportunities where you can find them."

Where he found his chance with Lucky Whitestone was in some swampy woods west of Tallahassee. Rand had tailed Whitestone off and on for most of those three years, either while on business in Tallahassee or on impromptu trips down from Atlanta.

"I knew he went hunting most Saturdays in the fall, and I knew where he went. On the day of his demise, I was already in the woods when he and his friends parked.

"I had gotten quite good with a long-range rifle, an item I bought from the estate of a well-to-do timber baron from Savannah, using a pseudonym, of course. What a great country we live in, Mr. Black, where you can purchase such a weapon and never have anyone know you bought it.

"I was at least 600 yards away when I blew his head off. I was rather proud of my marksmanship. It's a shame that Mr. Whitestone didn't suffer more, but it was important that I do the least risky procedure that would send him to hell. And at least I deprived him of the posthumous pleasure of an open casket.

"He was not, it turns out, very 'Lucky' at all."

Rand ticks off the others.

He had to travel less than two hours north of Atlanta to stake out Rabbit Larue. He took two years to cross Larue off the list. The old second baseman was something of a loner, but Finlay Rand befriended him by buying him Knob Creek on the rocks a couple of times at a honky-tonk bar where Rand was surprised they even carried it. Rand mentioned, a few drinks in, a fine stand of wacky weed that he was growing on a private patch down a side path off the Appalachian Trail. Larue needed money and did not think every law needed obeying, so an offer to help Rand harvest and then prepare the stuff for distribution later was met with cautious enthusiasm.

Larue met him at the trailhead and led him down the side path, where he says he beat his brains out with a large rock.

"Oh, it was a mess. I had the foresight to leave a shovel nearby earlier, and it took hours to give Mr. Larue an improper burial. I suppose some day a bear or a coyote will dig up his bones, if they haven't already."

With Paul "Boney" Bonesteel, it was just a matter of finding the right time. By this point, Rand had moved to New Jersey and opened a shop in the lower end of Manhattan. He had tracked Bonesteel and knew he was, unlike most of his former teammates, pretty good at making a buck with something other than a bat and a glove. He followed Bonesteel from the city to his large suburban home on Long Island several times over a period of three years before he finally found the right circumstances: an empty platform, an oncoming train.

"I'm surprised someone on the train didn't see me walking away just as Mr. Bonesteel was merging with the Long Island Rail Road."

The deaths of Jack Velasquez three years later and Jackson "The Ripper" Rittenbacker five years after that were simply a matter of managing to insinuate himself onto first a boat off the coast of Florida and then one on Lake Michigan. It involved a fair amount of traveling but, as Rand points out, folks in his business travel a lot.

"People are so willing to come to the aid of a distressed sailor," Rand says. "And the Atlantic Ocean and our Great Lakes are very large and convenient places for dumping trash."

The fact that Velasquez was found floating in several pieces didn't really surprise anyone. As Rand and many others knew, Jack Velasquez consorted with people who could turn murder into a creative art form. And everyone assumed that Rittenbacker just fell out of his boat and drowned.

"And then came my only failure so far, although I suppose I can only get half credit for your friend."

He traveled to North Carolina several times and became familiar with the too-predictable patterns of Buck McRae.

"He came out of that bar at the same time every night. I only had to drive up perhaps half an hour beforehand, and there was usually no one else in the lot.

"I thought I had killed him, but a moving target on a dark night was too much for me."

Rather than try again to kill the old right fielder, Rand moved on. He spent a couple of years in northern California, where he did a thriving business selling colonial antiques that seemed older on the West Coast than they had back east. He was there, though, for Roy Haas.

"This was my finest hour," he says. "If the list had been complete, I would have retired after that one."

Among the many wealthy and sometimes eccentric individuals Rand came in contact with as a major-league antiques dealer was a man living in King George County on Virginia's Northern Neck, near the Potomac. He few from San Francisco to Washington because the man, whom he had met before, said he had something no one else in the world had. He wouldn't tell Rand what it was. Rand was intrigued.

"He was old-school CIA, and he wanted to sell me some artifacts that had come into his hands. They were fairly worthless, many of them tied to John Wilkes Booth and his cohorts, for whom Mr. Cheatham had an unpleasant and unnatural affection. I was not impressed."

But then he told Rand that he had something that might be more rare than any of the furniture in his hilltop home with views of two rivers.

"He started telling me about a particularly wicked assassination the CIA had pulled off, involving a sort of dart gun that implanted a frozen poison into the bloodstream. The murder implement literally melts.

"And then, he got a strange gleam in his eye, and he told me he had one, and that he knew how to produce the poison and use it."

Rand smiles.

"Maybe he saw me as a kindred spirit, or maybe it was because he was old. He was starting to lose his memory, and he had, I think, alienated himself from the rest of his family. Whatever the reason, he traded this blatantly illegal instrument to me, only knowing that there was someone I wanted dead, and he showed me how to create the frozen poison bullet. It hurt me, Mr. Black, to part with $75,000 in cold, hard cash, but this was too good to pass up."

Rand originally had something more mundane planned for Roy Haas, but a gun that fired a poison dart that melted? He couldn't turn it down. Four years after he failed to kill Buck McRae, it was good-bye, Roy Haas.

"He was on his knees, trying to install a piece of carpet, when I found my chance. I explained who I was and why I was there to kill him. I'm not sure he understood my mission. He pretended to not even remember Frannie. After I shot him, I duct-taped his mouth to keep him from making too much noise until the poison took effect."

Rand says he stuck around the Sacramento area for a couple of days and even drove by the apartment where Roy Haas died.

"And then I moved to Richmond."

He got to know Les Hacker's habits. Rand was getting careless by this point, I guess, and arrogant. Nut jobs like Rand, the kind who believe they're smarter than everyone else and will never be caught, get that way. He said that, when he realized Les showed up in Monroe Park most days, he managed to buy a unit overlooking the park. Wasn't that damn hard, the way prices plummeted after the housing market sank like a stone.

"It was just too delicious. I could dispatch this one right from my living room window."

He says it like it's a goddamn game. I would give my 401(k) to get my hands around his well-tanned neck for a few seconds. I have no doubt that Finlay Rand stopped thinking of people as people a long time ago.

He says the little scorecards he sent in the mail every time to each of the present or future deceased or their next of kin were just part of the game.

"I wondered if any of them or their loved ones would figure it out, but no one ever did. People constantly disappoint me."

Rand looks down at his watch.

"I feel a sense of regret that there is one player left, Mr. Black, but time is running out. And maybe my misstep was a sign. Maybe the gods just did not want Buck McRae just yet. I hope, though, that poor Frannie will be satisfied with what I have accomplished."

He turns to look at me.

"When I say time is running out, I'm not just referring to my Biblical three-score and ten. My doctor tells me I have pancreatic cancer. It's particularly effective, and my life already is drifting into the land of diminishing returns. Time to take control."

He pulls out the pistol.

"I'll tell you what," he says. "I'll give you a fair chance."

He fishes a penny out of his pants pocket.

"Heads, I use this first bullet on myself, and you get to write the most amazing story of what I imagine is a mediocre and star-crossed career. Tails, you go first, and whoever finds us here hopefully discovers the tape recorder I've been using for the last hour."

He holds it up and smiles.

"Either way, the world finds out what I did for Frannie. The world finds out that evil is not always allowed to run rampant, with no consequences."

He places the penny on his thumb and flips it. I see it glint in the dim light. He catches it and turns my way. He shows me the coin. I guess I'm not going to win that Pulitzer.

"I'm sorry, Mr. Black. It looks as if you go first."

Chapter Twenty

*M*y only hope seems to be that Custalow will come looking for me before Finlay Rand pulls the trigger. If I could get this damn gag off, I think I could scream loud enough to penetrate even the brick walls of the Prestwould. Fat chance of that, though.

Rand, like he could read my mind, says, "Well, it's only a matter of time until that big oaf you live with comes looking for you."

Then he seems to have an inspiration.

"I know," he says, "we'll do it at that baseball stadium. What a nice way to tie everything up all nice and tidy, don't you think? Plus, I hate to mess up the apartment. The cleaning lady would be so upset."

He actually giggles. He sounds like this is some kind of damn caper, something we'll laugh about later. But, since Finlay Rand is holding a loaded gun and death delayed could be death denied, I nod my head.

"That's the boy," he says.

He blindfolds me and ties something around my ankles so I can't run, then jerks me out of the chair and leads me down the hall. With me shackled, it takes awhile. I can tell that we've gone past the front door. When he turns left into what my nose tells me is the kitchen, I know where we're going: the service elevator.

It can take us all the way down to the basement, without anyone hearing or seeing us. I hear it creak and wheeze its way toward us. Rand pushes me inside. I stumble and fall.

"I'm sorry, Mr. Black," I hear him say as he helps me up, "but we must hurry."

No need to apologize, I want to say. You're only going to kill me. Being a psychopath is never having to say you're sorry.

I think I can hear the other main elevator as we descend, no doubt Custalow coming, too late, to my rescue. Oh, well. It's the effort that counts.

On a weekday, someone might have been down here. Custalow perhaps, checking on the boiler. But it's Sunday, and Rand leads me, unchallenged and one halting foot at a time, up the steep steps. I can see daylight through the blindfold. Then, we're on level ground, the alley behind the Prestwould.

"The car's only a few feet away, Mr. Black," he says, poking me in the ribs with the instrument of my demise as we stumble along. I remember that Rand's Lexus is, damn the luck, just across the alley from the building.

Maybe, I think, Abe will break into Rand's unit and, eventually, look out the window and see what's becoming of me. But you can't see the alley from Rand's unit, and "eventually" probably would be too late anyhow.

Then, I'm in the car, pushed down in the back seat.

It takes all of five minutes, way too fast, before I feel us turning into what must be The Diamond's parking lot.

"Ah," I hear my captor say, "that'll do." He parks, yanks me out of the car and leads me, stumbling, through what seems like a small opening. I have to turn sideways to get through. We take a few more steps and then stop.

"Et voilà!" I hear Rand say as he rips off the blindfold.

We are in foul territory down the right field line, not far from the bullpen. It isn't, all things considered, a bad place to die.

"So it all ends where it began," Rand says. "Right where those animals played their stupid games. Frannie probably walked right where we're walking."

I see him pull the pistol out of the pocket of the $800 jacket he's chosen to spatter with our blood.

Then I see my salvation, walking on tiptoes, carrying what appears to be a thirty-three-ounce Louisville Slugger.

Jumpin' Jimmy Deacon's world is pretty much confined to The Diamond, as it once was to Parker Field. He doesn't really have much of a life away from the ballpark. He never married, and doesn't seem to have a lot of hobbies.

At his age, he should be working shorter hours. I know the Flying Squirrels wouldn't mind if he cut back a little. They probably sit around and wonder how they can get rid of the old goat without pissing off the whole city. Jimmy's become kind of a mascot. You might offend fewer people by pulling down Robert E. Lee's statue than by deep-sixing the baseball team's oldest and most faithful minion.

I owe much to Jumpin' Jimmy's devotion to baseball.

"Willie," he says, "is this the one?"

I nod like a bobblehead doll as Rand turns and fires one shot just as Jumpin' Jimmy catches him on the chin with a home-run swing.

Jimmy saw us from the time the car rolled up, it turns out. No math major, Jimmy still was able to put two and two together, and I'm glad I told him as much as I had earlier about Finlay Rand's vendetta against the 1964 Richmond Vees.

He likes to carry a bat with him as he makes the rounds, like a baseball nut's walking cane. He said he just likes the feel of it in his hand. This day, he has chosen a Chris Davis model, which he proceeds to use with great enthusiasm on Finlay Rand. His first swing leveled Rand, whose pistol went flying.

"Is this the asshole that shot Les?" he asks me. I nod. Maybe I shouldn't have, because that's Jimmy's signal to begin batting practice.

I might have tried to stop him if my hands had been free. I might have tried to persuade Jimmy to let the courts take care of Finlay Rand if I hadn't been gagged. I might have.

The way it works out, all I can do is stand here, hand-cuffed, shackled and gagged, and watch Jimmy administer justice with a Louisville Slugger to Rand's various body parts. It isn't a pretty sight. He doesn't stop until an overly enthusiastic swing causes the bat to splinter.

Rand's blood is seeping into the dirt. He hasn't moved since the second blow to the head.

Finally, Jimmy puts down the blood-stained bat remnant. He walks over and takes the gag off, then undoes my legs. He finds the key to the handcuffs in Rand's pocket.

"Jesus Christ, Jimmy," I say while he's unlocking me, "you didn't have to kill the son of a bitch."

He looks at me like I'm speaking in tongues.

"He shot Les," he says. "Jumpin' Jimmy doesn't believe in no half-ass measures."

Chapter Twenty-One

MONDAY

The church is packed. Someone managed to get a video feed set up in the community room for the overflow. Who knew Les Hacker had so many friends? I don't remember seeing a big line of people going in and out of Peggy's place when he was alive.

But who am I to judge? How many times have I seen some old acquaintance embalmed and looking like he's ready for the wax museum and realized that I really liked that guy, had some great times with him once upon a time, but hadn't called him in two years?

The place is nearly full by the time Peggy and I, Andi, Awesome Dude, and Les's brother and niece from Wisconsin, are led in. Walking up that aisle is like taking a trip back through my misspent life.

There are Abe and Andy Peroni and R. P. McGonnigal, who have known me since we were in single digits. Sitting next to Andy and his wife, I'm glad to see, is Cindy. This may mean nothing, but Cindy's not being here would definitely have meant something. There are other old faces from Oregon Hill. I even catch a glimpse of Walker Johnson, who seems likely to avoid much if any jail time for his much-applauded assault. I hear they've started a legal defense fund for him on the Hill. Put me down for fifty bucks.

On the other side of the aisle, I spy Mal Wheelwright, Sarah Goodnight, Sally Velez, Enos Jackson and a few other folks from the newspaper. For the most part, they didn't know Les, so I feel that drinks all around on me are in order in the near future.

Clara Westbrook, Louisa and Fred Baron, Patti and Pete Garland, Marcia the manager and some others from the Prest-would are here, too. This hasn't been a great time to live inside the old gray lady, with all the unwelcome publicity the place has gotten. Although, hell, it'll probably add to resale value. If the old saw about some publicity being better than none is true, Finlay Rand might have made everyone in the place a little richer, on paper at least.

And you have the Former Wives contingent. Jeanette and Glenn and their boys have come. So has Kate, accompanied by Mr. Ellis and by Marcus Green, whose grieving demeanor belies the fact that he never met Les.

The Oregon Hill crowd is in the majority, but there are many faces I don't know. I'll discover later the anonymous (until now) good turns Les did for many of them over the years. Cast your bread upon the waters, and they'll come to your funeral.

The service itself is something of an anticlimax. I am glad I suggested that the minister invite others to speak of Les. I go first and manage to get almost all the way through without breaking up. R. P. steps up, and then Awesome surprises me and everyone and says a few mangled words.

"Les treated me like I was somebody," Awesome says. After a silence that is drifting into uncomfortable, he adds, "That's all."

More people want to speak than get a chance. I see the minister glance at his watch.

Finally, it's over, and we can join the crowd already in the community room, probably already chowing down on the funeral feast in there.

Jumpin' Jimmy Deacon isn't here. We expect him to be out on bond by tomorrow. Marcus has already agreed to be his lawyer.

Finlay Rand is not dead. He should be, with the clubbing Jimmy gave him, but he still has a pulse. They don't expect him to make it. If he does, they're pretty sure he'll have an IQ somewhere between a squash and a rutabaga. I hope he'll be sentient enough to suffer.

Somebody called the cops, and a gunshot and severe clubbing along the right field line at The Diamond got their attention. They came charging up, all piss and vinegar. While we waited for them, Jimmy had a few questions.

"So he was really her brother?" he asked me.

"Can't you see the resemblance?"

Jimmy squinted, trying to find some remnant of Frannie Fling in the tenderized lump of human meat in front of him.

"I guess so. He must of had a hard time. But that didn't give him any right to shoot Les. That was uncalled-for."

He had picked up that splinter from the bat, out of habit I guess, and was still holding when the cops came busting in. It turned out that I had a slight concussion, but I was alert enough to make it clear to the horde of police that Jimmy had saved my life by clubbing Rand. The cops could tell that Rand had been hit many times with a baseball bat and thought Jimmy was perhaps a little too enthusiastic in his heroism.

I told them how full of crap they were for taking him off to jail, and they damn near arrested me instead of sending me to the hospital. I'm not supposed to head butt anybody for a couple of weeks.

As they were putting me into the ambulance, one of the cops asked me what was going on between me and the nearly deceased anyhow. What were we doing out here on an off day? I suspect, because cops have learned to expect the seamiest explanation possible, that he's imagining the worst, or at least the most salacious. Night cops reporter, antiques dealer and baseball lifer involved in sex triangle.

"Why don't you ask the chief?" I asked the cop as they shut the ambulance doors.

L. D. Jones is already playing defense. He knows I'm going to write, and soon, about how unresponsive he was to my earlier misgivings about Raymond Gatewood as a sniper. He held a press conference this morning to tell the TV mouth breathers that the department had been pursuing an alternative theory to Les Hacker's shooting, acting on a tip from an unnamed source, and that Finlay Rand might have panicked, knowing that the authorities were closing in on him.

Yeah, right. Sarah covered the press conference for the paper, as I was in the process of getting out of the hospital, and asked as many uncomfortable questions as she could. Oh, L. D. When are you going to listen to me?

Jones made it clear that, based on the tape that police found at the scene of the crime, Rand was involved in several other felonies. Sarah inquired as to whether they were all in the Richmond area. I had briefed her, from the hospital, so she knew all the answers before she asked the questions.

"We aren't at liberty to say," the chief said.

"Did some of them happen in Florida, Alabama, California and New York, among other states?"

So L. D. knew that I'd told her everything. All he could do was sputter and claim "ongoing investigation" while the TV types turned their cameras from the chief to Sarah, who told them to buzz off and do their own work.

That damn tape. By the time I thought of it, the cops had already stumbled on it in Rand's apartment and claimed it as their own. I'm sure they'll have a great time taking credit for all this, but the handful of people who still read the newspaper will know better. L. D. wants to talk to me, but by the time we talk, I guaran-damn-tee you my version will be in print.

I just wish I could have that tape. I'm working on memory. Bootie Carmichael used to tell me about one of our former sportswriters who had total recall. He could do a forty-five-minute interview without taking a note and quote it back verbatim. When a college football coach called him on it, after saying something he wished he hadn't and then reading it in the next day's paper, they told the sportswriter to pretend to take notes.

That guy ain't me. I have the gist of it, though, and I have all those interviews leading up to this. All over the country, next of kin are going to find out what really happened to their dearly beloveds, and why.

Peggy is still reeling a little, trying to take all this in. She's staying fairly smoked-up most of the time. What else is new? She understands that some nut who had it in for a long-ago minor-league baseball team shot Les Hacker just because his name happened to be on the opening-day lineup card. I'm not sure she really understands about Frannie Fling and all the rest. I'll have time to explain that later.

I called Grubby while I was still in the hospital. Sandy McCool put me through to him right away, which told me that my publisher was, for once, eager to talk to me.

I assume he still reads his paper. The story was on B1 this morning. Sarah wrote it. She was off and probably hung over, but she got word via one of our Facebook friends about nine cop cars converging on The Diamond and was on it like white on rice, long before anybody called Chuck Apple, the Sunday cops guy. The story had some pretty shapely legs. Reporter abducted. Local baseball lifer beats wealthy antiques dealer nine-tenths to death. "Reporter abducted" probably doesn't elicit much of a response from our readers, beyond "good," but the rest of it was much more moist than the dry toast we usually try to serve our readers on Monday mornings. Sarah followed the ambulance to the hospital, where I told her everything I wanted to relay to our readers.

I told Grubby he might want to bump the paper up a few pages on Tuesday, and that he might want to take this one from sports for A1. When I told him all the gory details, the kind of details that sells papers, I could practically hear his drool hitting the phone. Grubby could use some good news, something to make those little numbers that rule his life do a U-turn and take at least a temporary turn upward. The best thing that could happen to the paper, just about everyone agrees, is for somebody to buy the damn thing and maybe uncouple it from the shit pile of bad-judgment debt the suits across the street have piled on us.

But Grubby is cautious. He doesn't dread losing a lawsuit. He dreads a lawsuit, period. Attorneys are expensive.

"We'll have to run this one by the lawyers."

I asked him why.

"None of this has been proven."

Proved, I silently tell Grubby. Jesus Christ, you used to be a reporter. Proven is an adjective.

Out loud, I tell him that every bit of it is true, and when the police release the information on the tape, they'll have Finlay Rand's full confession, murder by murder.

"Well, we might have to wait until they release it. We can write something for tomorrow, but we have to be careful."

You shouldn't call your publisher a nitwit. It isn't good business. However, I was slightly concussed and a little bit mainstream pissed off. I explained to Grubby, in fairly graphic terms, what assholes we'd look like if we sat on all this material and waited for the cops to dribble it out, probably to the TV stations first, a drop at a time.

He said he ought to suspend me. I said maybe he should, but that it would be in his best interests to run this damn story in the Tuesday paper before he did that.

He said, finally, to go ahead and write it, and we would try to get it past the lawyers.

I don't think Grubby likes me very much right now, but that's OK. It's reciprocal.

And so, after Les's funeral, and after spending an hour or so with my mother and all the rest of the people mourning Les

Hacker's passing, I am going in to the paper to write the truth. The truth doesn't always get printed, but you've got to try.

Kate came by the hospital last night. She saw it on the six o'clock news. It's amazing they had it. If anyone's more short-staffed on Sundays than newspapers, it's TV newsrooms.

She showed some compassion for my aching head, but her main interest seemed to be in how this is going to play out for Raymond Gatewood. And, as usual, she found my willingness to share information somewhat below the acceptable level.

"You always do this," she said, as the nurse came in and told her to keep her voice down or leave.

"You never share. You didn't share back then, and you're not sharing now. What's wrong with you, Willie?"

She seemed near tears, which I partially attributed to the fact that there's a fetus kicking field goals inside her.

"We could have been so good. We were so good."

I note that things seem to be working out well for her. Husband, baby, a job doing real lawyering instead of helping corporations screw the rest of us.

She wipes a tear away and tells me I should walk a mile in her shoes.

I tell her I tried that at one of Clara Westbrook's Halloween costume parties, and it did not go well.

She lets go with a grudging laugh, and we have a special moment, remembering some of the good stuff that made the rest bearable. Truth is, neither one of us was willing to be the gardener, tending to the hard stuff while the other one bloomed like a rose. If I were a better person, the gardener would have been me. I mean, Kate probably will make three times what I do by the time she quits working.

I tell her everything I've learned about Finlay Rand's misadventures. By the time I'm through, she feels as certain as I do that Mr. Gatewood will be breathing the cool, clean air of Monroe Park in the not-too-distant future. Oh, they'll probably try to hang some kind of bullshit on him, but with Kate and Marcus Green as his lawyers, they would be well-advised to just let the man go and hope he doesn't sue the police department for too much.

In the brief time I have after the funeral before duty calls, I see a familiar but unexpected face in the crowd. There, accompanied by Lydia, is Buck McRae, looking very uncomfortable in a suit and clip-on tie.

Lydia insisted on coming up to Richmond with Buck, probably to keep him out of trouble. Couldn't keep him away.

I pull Buck to one side and bring him up to speed on yesterday's festivities at The Diamond.

"So the fella, the one that you said shot me, he's not going to be doing anybody else any harm?"

I assure Buck that Finlay Rand won't be doing anyone any harm, now or ever. About the only harm he can impart now is if, either in his current vegetative state or in the aftermath of his much-deserved death, he causes Jimmy Deacon to serve any real jail time.

It's difficult to see how the world could come down very hard on Jumpin' Jimmy. Yeah, he took a few extra cuts when he was doing BP on Rand's head, but I'm sure Marcus Green can make it look like the actions of a man driven by fear and the sight of his good friend (me) in considerable peril. By the time Marcus is through, the jury might vote to build Jimmy a statue on Monument Avenue, maybe a couple of blocks west of the one of Arthur Ashe. Instead of a tennis racket, Jimmy's statue would be wielding a thirty-three-ounce Louisville Slugger.

Cindy breaks away from the impromptu Hill homecoming, where everybody realizes they haven't seen each other since the last funeral, and is standing beside me. Buck and Lydia move away, and I turn, not sure what I should say.

I start to speak. She shushes me.

"You look like hell," she says. I'm sure I do, with my noggin slightly misshapen and my raccoon eyes.

I wait. Nothing I will say right now is going to make this any better. I know Cindy Peroni well enough to understand that whatever she's decided, she's decided.

"You let me down," she says. "I told you I wasn't going to go through any more pain not of my own making. Didn't I tell you that?"

I nod. Yes, she did.

Then I feel her take my right hand in her left one.

"I know this is a hard day for you," she says, "but I had to say that. I didn't want to just leave it out there and us pretend that we never met, never, well, you know . . ."

I know. I could promise Cindy that I'll never let alcohol screw things up again. I could promise that I'll try really, really hard this time to stop smoking. The other thing I could promise, that it'll just be me and her forever, would be much easier to keep than the first two.

But I know, and she knows, what promises are worth.

"The crazy thing is, I'm still attracted to you. I still care about you. Maybe, one day when I'm weaker than I am right now, we can try it again. But I don't know."

Fair enough. No promises on either side, just a teaspoon of hope.

She squeezes my hand and walks away. I watch to see if she'll look back. She doesn't.

I walk over to where Peggy is sitting in a chair, a queen holding court. She's taken a dope holiday and looks like she could use a hit right now. In a sane world, she'd be able to sit there, toking away, while she told everyone stories about Les. As it is, she seems to be holding up pretty well. She tells them how he was the best thing that ever happened to her ("except for this one," she says, grabbing me and pulling me to her), how he never seemed to be in a bad mood, how despite the fact that he could have handled any of her other "pissant" husbands and boyfriends "two at a time," he never even threatened to hurt anyone, no matter how much they provoked him.

"And, after he got, you know, kind of forgetful, he just got more sweet."

Andi is standing by her and leans down to give her grand-mom a buss on the cheek. For some reason, one of the neighbors has brought a camera, and she wants to take our picture. Hell of a time for that, I'm thinking, but Peggy's OK with it.

I don't know if we should be smiling. It seems kind of inappropriate, but Peggy and Andi give it their best shot, so I do the same and hope I don't break the camera. I wonder what this photo is going to look like and hope it doesn't wind up on Facebook.

I've been carrying the picture of Frannie Fling, née Frances Flynn, around in my wallet since Jumpin' Jimmy gave it to me. I look at it now. The photograph is getting a little worn around the edges, as if Jimmy might have taken it out once or twice or a few hundred times. Still, you can see the life there, the spark.

You can see how little Dairy Flynn might have been driven to do what he did, become the monster he became, if nature and nurture already were pointing him toward hell. I don't really believe in pure evil, but I do believe some people fight the varying levels of evil within us a lot harder than others do. I think about how a thoughtless act almost half a century ago has led me to Les Hacker's funeral today. As the perpetrator of a lifetime of thoughtless acts myself, it is almost too much to bear.

I lean over and give Peggy a hug. Andi walks me to the door, and I give her one, too.

I close the door on what is threatening to turn into the kind of party Les would have wanted everyone to have. I reach for a cigarette.

Silence follows me down the long hall, broken only by my own footsteps.

I have a story to write.